THE WOMAN WITHOUT A SHADOW

A Twice-Told Tale

HUGO VON HOFMANNSTHAL

Introduction by Dana Gioia

Translated from the German by Vincent Kling

Wiseblood Books

WISEBLOOD BOOKS
Joshua Hren, Editor-in-Chief
Post Office Box 870
Menomonee Falls, WI 53052
www.wisebloodbooks.com

Printed in the United States of America

CONTENTS

Introduction

BY DANA GIOIA

Years ago I had a long conversation with a fellow writer about modern German literature. We spoke of Thomas Mann, Franz Kafka, Hermann Hesse, Rainer Maria Rilke, and Bertolt Brecht. Then we discussed the last writers of the Habsburg empire—Hermann Broch, Stefan Zweig, Georg Trakl, and Robert Musil. It was a rare pleasure to compare opinions with someone who loved German literature as much as I did. Late in the evening I asked if he had ever read Hugo von Hofmannsthal. My friend recognized the name but confessed he had never read anything. Was this the poet, he inquired, who had written the libretto for Richard Strauss's *Der Rosenkavalier*?

Then he put me on the spot. What American writer did Hofmannsthal resemble? I thought for a moment and replied, "Imagine a mixture of Thornton Wilder, T. S. Eliot, and Nathaniel Hawthorne." It was a formulation too clever to be useful. I admitted defeat and said the obvious. There was no one like Hofmannsthal in American literature. There wasn't even anyone like him in German literature. Hofmannsthal was the citizen of that notional region called *Mitteleuropa*. It wasn't a nation or vanished empire but a state of mind—the collective anxiety of Central European societies caught between the East and West. Its capital was the city that made neurosis famous—Vienna.

In America, Hofmannsthal is known, if at all, only by operagoers. Four of his six collaborations with Strauss hold a place in the operatic repertory—*Elektra* (1909), *Der Rosenkavalier*

(1911), *Ariadne auf Naxos* (1912, rev. 1916), and *Die Frau ohne Schatten* (1919). It would be hard to imagine four operas more different from one another than that remarkable quartet. Together with several verse plays, most notably *Jedermann* (1911), a version of the medieval morality play *Everyman,* these works establish Hofmannsthal as one of few major poetic dramatists of the last century. Given the international presence of his operatic works, he ranks as the most widely performed verse dramatist of his era.

Hofmannsthal wrote in German, but he isn't best understood as a German author. He was quintessentially Viennese—polyglot, Catholic, Jewish, and cosmopolitan. He was a product of the multicultural Austro-Hungarian Empire and its sophisticated capital Vienna. Unlike the newly unified Germany with its aggressive sense of national identity, the dual monarchy of Austria and Hungary represented an older political vision. The Habsburg emperors aspired to be stern but loving parents to an unruly family of a dozen nations and ethnic groups. They bragged that their dynasty had been built by royal alliances rather than conquest. The unofficial dynastic motto was, *"Bella gerant alii, tu felix Austria, nube."* ("Let others wage war, you, happy Austria, marry.") It was not a political system that could survive the First World War; it fell to pieces before the Armistice. Yet in its long and delicately balanced heyday, it had created a diverse and sophisticated culture unlike any other in Europe.

Habsburg Austria had nourished great artists for centuries. Its musical culture was unsurpassed, producing Wolfgang Amadeus Mozart, Franz Josef Haydn, Franz Schubert, Gustav Mahler, Anton Bruckner, Arnold Schoenberg, Erich Wolfgang Korngold, and Alban Berg. In the visual arts and architecture, there were Gustav Klimt, Oskar Kokoschka, Egon Schiele, Adolf Loos, and Otto Wagner. Modern Austrian literature included Broch, Musil, Trakl, Zweig, Arthur Schnitzler, and Karl Kraus. The city also nurtured an innovative intellectual milieu with talents as various as Sigmund Freud, Ludwig Wittgenstein, Theodor Herzl, and Ludwig von Mises.

Born in 1874, Hugo Laurenz August Hofmann Edler von Hofmannsthal embodied the international heritage of the Habsburg Empire. His mother was a Catholic Austrian. His father was also Catholic, a mix of Austrian and Italian. The family money and aristocratic title, however, dated back to the poet's paternal great-grandfather, Isaak Low Hofmann, a tobacco merchant and Jewish leader, who had been ennobled by the emperor. When T. S. Eliot spoke of a poet possessing "the mind of Europe," he could have been describing Hofmannsthal. The Austrian poet not only knew Latin, Greek, French, English, Spanish, and Italian in addition to his native German; he had read deeply in all of those literatures.

Hofmannsthal's career was not merely unusual but singular. He began publishing at sixteen. He used a pseudonym since high school students were not allowed to publish. No one realized that the perfect poems printed under the name "Loris" were written by a teenager. Within a year, Hofmannsthal was a celebrated poet. His literary precocity is unique in German literature. As Stefan Zweig observed in his memoir, *The World of Yesterday* (1942):

> The appearance of the young Hofmannsthal is and remains notable as one of the greatest miracles of accomplishment early in life . . . I know no other youthful example of a similar impeccability in the

mastering of language, no such breadth of spiritual buoyancy, nothing more permeated with poetic
substance even in the most casual lines, than in this
magnificent genius, who already in his sixteenth and
seventeenth year had inscribed himself in the eternal
annals of the German language with unextinguish-
able verses and prose which today has still not been
surpassed.

Hofmannsthal's sudden youthful emergence recalls the
explosive debut of Arthur Rimbaud, though Hofmannsthal,
secure in his education and affluence, had the stability to
sustain his artistic development impossible to his doomed
French counterpart. While Hofmannsthal was still in second-
ary school, Stefan Georg, the influential German Symbolist
poet, came to Vienna to enlist the teenage author in his aesthetic movement. Few poets have had so early and effortless
a rise to fame.

In his twenties Hofmannsthal wrote verse plays, essays,
poems, and stories. He was a leading figure in the Viennese
fin de siècle renaissance, the bard of *Jung Wien,* a group of pro-
gressive young writers who gathered at the Café Griensteidl.
The *Jung Wein,* which included Zweig, Schnitzler, and Kraus,
disagreed on aesthetics and politics, but they shared an antip-
athy toward naturalism. As Zweig attests, the other members
of Young Vienna were in awe of Hofmannsthal's genius; none
of them had yet achieved anything comparable, but his success
filled them with hope for their own future.

Then in 1902 Hofmannsthal made an extraordinary decision—he abandoned poetry. It was not a case of waning
inspiration or changing interests. Vienna's leading young poet

had undergone a philosophical crisis. Hofmannsthal became disillusioned with poetry's ability to express reality. "No direct path leads from poetry to life," he wrote, "nor does any lead from life to poetry." Hofmannsthal presented his dilemma in a short story, *Ein Brief* ("The Letter"). Now generally known as "The Lord Chandos Letter," this fictional epistle adopts the voice of an Elizabethan aristocrat writing to Sir Francis Bacon. It describes the emotional and intellectual crisis of a twenty-six-year-old writer who has abandoned literature because of its inability to convey the reality of human thought and experience. The young aristocrat sees this failure not only in his own work but in the entire edifice of literature from the ancient classics to the present.

Hofmannsthal was twenty-six when he published the Chandos letter. Few critics missed the autobiographical nature of the work. Now considered a foundational text of European modernism, this prophetic essay deconstructs the Symbolist notion of lyric poetry. It claims that the alluring structures of literary language that enchant the senses were too self-referential. Language connected to itself rather than the outer world. Poetry was not only insufficient in conveying reality; its elegant forms and intoxicating sound confused and obscured meaning. Hofmannsthal's "estrangement from lyricism," to use Hermann Broch's phrase, wasn't an aesthetic or political decision; it was an epistemological necessity. In the words of John Banville, "the world-that-we-speak was no longer the world-as-it-is."

The Chandos letter was the turning point of Hofmannsthal's literary career. He resolved to escape the interiority and subjectivity of poetry for the communal and physical art of drama. This decision is often portrayed as the poet's need for a direct relationship with an audience, but that motivation was only partially true. Hofmannsthal also recognized the energy and clarity that came from collaboration with other artists—composers, designers, directors, actors, singers, and dancers. The subjectivity of the poet could be corrected by the transformative energy of collaboration. The obfuscations of language could also be clarified in the physical reality of performance; wordless gesture and movement could convey meanings beyond words. "A pure gesture," he wrote in his essay "On Pantomime" (1911), "is like a pure thought that has been stripped even of the momentarily witty, the restrictedly individual, and the grotesquely characteristic." The performer embodies the words and music of the theatrical work so that it communicates to the audience as "a human whole that speaks to the whole."

Hofmannsthal's choice of theater also had theological motivation. As critic Alfred Schwarz observed, Hofmannsthal had decided that "his imagination demanded a symbolic stage, a theater like medieval-Elizabethan or Calderon's." He envisioned a style of drama that expressed great themes played under the eyes of God. Such an ambition, Schwarz notes, "demanded the allegorical mode." Hofmannsthal wanted to revive a Catholic form of theater that could communicate the mysteries of existence. It rejected the Realist emphasis on the unique nature of individual experience, circumstance, and personality; it sought to represent universal truths through representative human types in symbolic narratives. In *The Salzburg Great Theater of the World*, for example, half the cast is supernatural: Death, World, two Angels, Adversary, and Master. The earthly cast is also allegorical: Kind, Beauty, Wisdom, Rich Man, Farmer, and Beggar. The mortals represent various types of humanity. As Schwarz suggests, the play enacts "the impalpable life of the soul; it tests the creature under the eyes of the creator."

Although Hofmannsthal continued to write fiction and criticism, the major works of his subsequent career were mostly dramatic. These include ambitious verse plays, most notably *Elektra* (1903), *Everyman* (1911), *The Salzburg Great Theater of the World* (1922), and *The Tower* (1925) as well as his prose comedy, *The Difficult Man* (1921). The artistic distinction of his spoken drama was matched by the six opera libretti he wrote for Strauss. These include his two final stage works, *The Egyptian Helena* (1928) and *Arabella* (1933), which was produced posthumously after Hofmannsthal's sudden death at fifty-five in 1929.

Hofmannsthal did not think of the libretto as an inferior artistic form; he saw opera as an important and distinct form of poetic theater. It was also a literary form that allowed an author freedom to explore visionary and symbolic material. He crafted his libretti with the same seriousness that went into his plays. No modern poet devoted comparable imaginative energy to operatic theater. Not since Richard Wagner (who wrote all of his own texts) had German opera had a librettist of such originality, literary quality, and cultural ambition.

Die Frau ohne Schatten (*The Woman without a Shadow*) was Hofmannsthal's fourth libretto for Strauss. When he first approached the composer in 1911 with the idea for a fairy tale opera, he described it in a manner designed to flatter Strauss. Hofmannsthal suggested that their hugely successful opera, *Der Rosenkavalier,* had been the modern equivalent of Mozart's *The Marriage of Figaro.* (For a composer to be compared to Mozart is a sort of deification.) Their new work, the poet promised him, would resemble *The Magic Flute*. "Not that there is any imitation in either case," Hofmannsthal added, "only a certain analogy." What Hofmannsthal had in mind was not the "enchanting naïveté" of Mozart's comic adventure but something darker.

The Woman without a Shadow has notable similarities to *The Magic Flute*. Both operas unfold in magical worlds, and each presents two romantic couples (one royal, the other common). Both plots involve a quest to resolve the obstacles to a happy union for the couples. Each opera ends in a series of ritual tests to purify the lovers. Both works also present an evil older woman who manipulates the characters. Despite these similarities, the two operas could hardly be less alike. *The Magic Flute* is animated by light-hearted adventure and low comedy, mixed with an elevated Masonic subplot. Mozart's couples experience love at first sight; their brief trials happen on the way to happy marriages. *The Magic Flute* is an opera about youthful love and courtship.

The Woman without a Shadow is a serious, passionate, and complex marital drama. It deals with mature issues of sex, secrecy, infidelity, and infertility, which are alien to Mozart's callow lovers. Even the comic elements in Hofmannsthal's libretto are grotesque. Rough and unpleasant humor is provided by Barak's three disabled brothers. The opera moves slowly with majestic music and violent emotionalism. In performance, the richly textured work seems closer to Wagner's "sacred festival" opera *Parsifal* than Mozart's Masonic comedy.

In *The Woman without a Shadow*, grave problems confront both couples. Only the women, however, know what is really happening; neither husband understands the peril of his situation. The first couple is both noble and supernatural.

The Emperor, a great hunter, has captured the shapeshifting daughter of Keikobad, the father-God. They marry, and she becomes his Empress. The two are not merely in love; they live in sustained erotic ecstasy. The exuberant Emperor has no idea that they also live under a curse; he is doomed unless his immortal wife conceives a child. (In folklore, there is mortal danger when a supernatural being crosses into the mortal realm.) Meanwhile, in the ordinary human world, Barak the Dyer loves his bored and resentful wife. A generous and open man, he strives to please her without success. He longs for children from the woman who bars him from her bed.

The two couples are surrounded by numerous other characters, both human and divine; the early scenes are crowded with action. Hofmannsthal's complex dramatic poem, however, has a simple, unifying plot. The Empress must obtain the shadow of a mortal woman to allow her to conceive a child and save her beloved husband. Barak's wife is willing to make the trade to obtain the pleasure, passion, and luxury missing from her life.

The central symbol of the opera (and the subsequent novella) is the female shadow. There are many nuances in Hofmannsthal's employment of the image, but its central meaning is clear. The shadow is the soul, the essence of humanity, which allows a woman both to love and create new life. For the Dyer's wife, losing her shadow not only ends her ability to have children; it also destroys the love she still bears her husband. To sell one's shadow is a demonic bargain that must end badly. The theme of diabolical dealing in *The Woman without a Shadow* is reinforced by the opera's allusions to Goethe's *Faust*. The most notable is the Empress's scheming and malevolent Nurse, who is a dour version of Goethe's

Mephistopheles. Hofmannsthal's story is both deeply Catholic and folkloric; the natural expression of sexual love is marriage and children. For Hofmannsthal, love is individually motivated, but its consummation brings lovers into the universal cycle of life.

Childbearing is an unusual theme for traditional opera. Some viewers find it a problematic premise for musical drama. Isn't opera better suited to depict the passions of romantic love than the complex burdens of marriage and parenthood? These questions are particularly puzzling today when many people do not consider marriage or family as personal priorities. Hofmannsthal's opera and novella unabashedly celebrate birth and motherhood but not in any narrow political sense. His natalism is existential and elemental.

The Woman without a Shadow ponders the primal importance of procreation. As Hannah Arendt declared, birth is "the miracle that saves the world, the realm of human affairs, from its normal 'natural' ruin." For her, new life not only provides the continuation but the renewal of humanity. For Hofmannsthal, birth redeems us from death; it is the bridge between the past and future. Despite the opera's sophisticated modernist form, its vision is primordial. The oldest myths are fertility stories; they depict the renewal of both the earth and its people. Whether or not one wants to be part of the cycle of procreation, it is a mistake to ignore the centrality of motherhood in culture. Childbearing is embedded in myth and folklore. The last sentence in French fairy tales, often omitted in English translations, is "they lived happily and had many children." The originality of Hofmannsthal's story is to put this biological necessity and folkloric theme at the center of his modern psychological drama.

Sexual desire is a standard theme for opera, both comic and tragic, but no librettist approached the subject with such philosophical, indeed even theological, passion as Hofmannsthal. In his libretti, he explores erotic love and its many manifestations in courtship, marriage, and infidelity. This was an obsession shared by Strauss, even before his collaborations with Hofmannsthal. In Strauss's early *Salome* (1905), based on Oscar Wilde's French-language play, sexuality is delusional, aggressive, and destructive. Each of Hofmannsthal and Strauss's operas presents different views of erotic love. *The Cavalier of the Rose*, which opens with a musical depiction of the sex act, begins in adultery and ephebophilia and ends in marriage between two young lovers. *Ariadne on Naxos* simultaneously depicts the tragic and comic aspects of the same romantic situation; erotic love is both a self-indulgent delusion and a divine transformation. *Arabella* presents the long delayed sexual awakening of two sisters, one outwardly repressed, the other inwardly. The most extreme example is *The Egyptian Helena*, which depicts betrayal, infidelity, magical deception, and marital reconciliation.

The most ambitious of all of Hofmannsthal's libretti, *The Woman without a Shadow* glorifies eroticism. Dangerous and uncontrollable, sexual love offers not only ecstasy and union but metamorphosis. The poet works in the baroque Catholic tradition in which eroticism acquires a mystical dimension. Love unifies the body and the soul. Sex is the purest expression of the life force uniting the past and future through new life. (A contemporary reader can't help noticing how Hofmannsthal's ideas adumbrate later discoveries of the transmission of DNA across generations.) At the end of act one, the night watchman sings to the couples in their beds, "Holy is your work of love." Sex is "the bridge / across the abyss / over which the dead / return to life."

The Woman without a Shadow had a long gestation. Hofmannsthal first suggested the subject in 1911. It was put aside while he and Strauss produced the first version of *Ariadne on Naxos* in 1912, which presented a spoken version of Molière's *The Bourgeois Gentleman* followed by an operatic divertissement. The mix of spoken and sung drama proved so impractical that they dropped the play entirely and created a completely operatic work only loosely based on Molière. This radical revision absorbed both artists for several years. They were also distracted with work on their ballet, *The Legend of Joseph* (1914). The outbreak of World War I further delayed the new project. When Strauss completed the score in 1916, he knew it would be impossible to stage until the war was over.

Finally, in 1919 *Die Frau ohne Schatten* had its premiere at Vienna's Staatsoper where Strauss had just been named the principal conductor. The creators hoped the opera would succeed on the scale of *Der Rosenkavalier*, but it had a mixed reception. Strauss's magnificent score proved difficult to sing; it required a stellar cast and a masterful conductor. Meanwhile the complexity of the libretto demanded skilled direction and strong production to keep the audience from confusion. After its initial stagings in Germany and Austria, *The Woman without a Shadow* retreated to the edge of the repertory. Only in the 1950s did it return, championed by Austrian conductor Karl Bohm. Slowly the opera became acknowledged as one of Strauss's masterpieces.

Hofmannsthal keenly felt the failure of *The Woman without a Shadow*. He considered the libretto one of his finest works—the realization of a new form of symbolic theater dramatizing his Catholic vision. Reviving spiritual theater was not an abstract fantasy for the poet. He had already begun planning, with Strauss and director Max Reinhardt, a new international arts festival in Salzburg. Supported by the local archbishop, the festival presented theater, opera, and music in an atmosphere that embodied the now vanished Habsburg traditions of multicultural inclusion and Catholic spirituality. (It deliberately set itself against the nationalism, secularism, and racism emerging in Germany.) The first Salzburg festival in 1920 opened with Reinhardt's production of Hofmannsthal's *Everyman.* Performed on the steps of the cathedral, the play had such success that it has been repeated in every subsequent festival. In 1921, concerts were added, and then in 1922, four of Mozart's operas were produced. It soon became evident that Hofmannsthal had helped create Europe's leading arts festival.

Now at the height of his fame and literary powers, Hofmannsthal again did something unexpected. He decided to rewrite *The Woman without a Shadow* as prose fiction. It is hard to overstate how radical a notion this was. Many classic operas have been based on prose works. *Carmen, Manon Lescaut, La Bohème*, and *Werther* are a few of many examples. Likewise, some successful operas have been adapted into fiction. Anthony Burgess rewrote *The Cavalier of the Rose* as a short story; *The Magic Flute* exists in numerous prose versions, mostly for children. To my knowledge, however, no poet has ever taken his or her own original opera libretto and reconceived it as a serious work of fiction. Hofmannsthal's project had an air of both desperation and defiance. He believed in the importance of his work. If audiences had found his libretto too complex and obscure as theater, the poet was determined to develop his material to clarify its meaning.

Two features of Hofmannsthal's prose version of *The Woman without a Shadow* may puzzle American readers. First, is the fairy tale the proper narrative mode for a serious work of modernist literature, especially one full of symbolism and psychological complexity? Second, why did Hofmannsthal choose the novella as his form? Wouldn't a short story, closer to the length of a traditional folktale, have offered greater clarity and compression? Or, for an extended narrative, wouldn't a novel have been the right form to provide more depth and detail? The answer to these questions is found in the German literary tradition.

The fairy tale has a stature in German literature difficult for Americans to understand. It is not a children's form relegated to the margins of literature; it is an essential part of the national literary tradition. Modern German literature developed later than the literatures of England, France, or Italy. Even as late as 1700, the German-speaking world was divided into hundreds of political entities—kingdoms, principalities, duchies, margraviates, bishoprics, and free cities—many associated with the Holy Roman Empire. There was no unified sense of national identity. For centuries there had not even been a common German language since different dialects were spoken across central Europe. Only after the Reformation did the Saxon-based New High German used by Martin Luther for his translation of the Bible provide the basis for a national language. It gave Germans a common written form, no matter what dialect they spoke locally. German identity began, therefore, as a shared literary experience—reading the Bible in the same, new, half-familiar, half-strange language, *Lutherdeutsch*.

Without political unity, the German people searched for national identity in their cultural heritage. Where could the true character of the German imagination be found? For many artists, the answer was in folk tales, called *Marchen* ("little stories") in German. These stories had been passed on by common people through the oral tradition. These folkloric tales, full of wonder and enchantment, often including suffering and violence, exercised a huge influence on German literature. They were collected and published in many versions by writers and scholars, most notably the brothers Jacob and Wilhelm Grimm. Folk tales provided a basis for serious literary composition. To a degree unparalleled in English, German authors have based stories, poems, novels, plays, and operas on folkloric forms and themes. In English, the fairy tale suggests children's literature; in German, it is a venerable narrative mode.

Hofmannsthal was drawn to the fairy tale because, unbound by the conventions of realism, it offered an ideal form for symbolic literature. Since the Romantic era, writers such as Novalis, Ludwig Tieck, Adelbert von Chamisso, and E. T. A. Hoffmann had composed serious works in the folkloric mode. (Hoffman's stories inspired Jacques Offenbach's 1881 *opera fantastique*, *Tales from Hoffmann.*) Anyone comparing nineteenth-century fiction in Germany, France, and England will notice how different the traditions are. While the characteristic works of French and English authors such as Balzac, Stendhal, Dickens, and Eliot are long realist novels, full of social detail and psychological portraiture, the classics of German fiction are mostly shorter tales full of youthful adventure or supernatural wonder. It is the fiction of poets drawn to romance rather than realism.

Even in the early twentieth century, the novella had not been eclipsed by the novel. It was the vehicle for many of the greatest works of modern German fiction such as Thomas Mann's *Tonio Kröger,* Franz Kafka's *The Metamorphosis*, and Hermann Hesse's *Siddhartha*. Hofmannsthal would have seen it as the obvious genre for retelling his fantastic libretto. The novella was also the favorite form of Hofmannsthal's lifelong friend, Stefan Zweig, whose works such as *The Royal Game*, *Amok*, and *Letter from an Unknown Woman* sold in the millions. Hofmannsthal looked down on Zweig's commercial narratives, but their success reminded him of the novella's continuing popularity.

Long fiction was not an easy form for Hofmannsthal. He spent twenty years struggling with his only novel, *Andreas*, which remained unfinished at his death. *The Woman without a Shadow* (1920) is the only piece of long prose fiction the poet ever completed. Writing the novella, he commented, was "the most difficult task I have ever undertaken." His exertion was understandable—the novella was not simply a prose version of the opera. Hofmannsthal reimagined the work; he expanded, elaborated, and transformed the material for the page. New scenes and characters appear. The larger mythical world becomes clearer. The inner lives of the main characters emerge in greater depth and detail. The opera's offstage chorus of unborn children becomes the basis of a new, extended episode that provides the spiritual center of the novella. Only in prose does Hofmannsthal fully explain his visionary tale of marriage, infidelity, redemption, and birth. The novella is so startling in its revelations that it transforms our interpretation of the opera.

Hofmannsthal's novella is an independent and complete work of art. The reader requires no familiarity with the opera to understand the tale. Yet anyone who knows the opera will notice how Hofmannsthal's prose style replicates the high emotional state of Strauss's music. The narrative style is subjective and lyric, quite unlike the detached expository method of most fairy tales. Mixing interior monologue and stream-of-consciousness technique, Hofmannsthal projects the inner lives of his characters, especially the feverish thoughts of the Empress as she plots to save her husband. The style and psychological focus of *The Woman without a Shadow* places it firmly in its historical moment, post-World War I Vienna—the literary milieu of Musil, Zweig, Schnitzler, and Freud.

Even with Hofmannsthal's relative neglect in America, it is astonishing the prose version of *The Woman without a Shadow* has never been completely translated into English. It is the major piece of prose fiction by one of the finest German-language writers of the last century. Fascinating in itself, it is also the key to understanding the most mysterious and ambitious of Strauss and Hofmannsthal's operas. The importance of Vincent Kling's new version of both the libretto and novella is self-evident. Here, at last, is a full account of Hofmannsthal's visionary twin masterworks of poetic drama and prose.

THE WOMAN WITHOUT A SHADOW

Novella

This translation is dedicated in loving memory to Andrew Coale

September 24, 1971 – February 14, 2018

Where words fail me, I can borrow those of the great
Hugo von Hofmannsthal.
He has shown me for most of my life the charge of wonder
and mystery in everyday life.

During our short time, you did the same for me, friend.
I saw you confront grief with courage,
sorrow with laughter,
losses with contemplative acceptance,
never seeking to run or deny.

Through solemnity and hilarity, you showed me
depths of spirit and heights of love.
Thank you for the trust of telling me about your father,
of bringing me into the warmth of your mother and step-father,
of sharing a gracious, easy wisdom
far beyond your years.

I see you now before me again—
(*Ihr naht euch wieder, schwankende Gestalten*)
—the smile, the warmth, the love, the sheer kindness,
and I say with reverence what the Empress
from the spirit world says about Barak:

Praise to him who saw to it
That I should find this one man among the rest,
For he shows me what true humanness is like,
And for his sake I want to remain with men and women
And breathe their breath and bear their hardships with them!

Chapter One

The Emperor was with the Empress, who in the heat of summer occupied a chamber on the topmost terrace of the blue palace. True to her habit, the Nurse was keeping vigilant watch outside the door, angrily brooding on the turn of fortune that had delivered her mistress, a spirit being and the jealously guarded daughter of the powerful Spirit King, into the hands of a mortal man to be his spouse, no matter that he was the Emperor of the Southeastern Islands. In her imagination she and the spirit child entrusted to her care were dwelling still, as so often in her fancy, on the remote little island around which flowed the ebony-black waters of a deep tarn encircled by the Seven Mountains of the Moon, where they had passed years in quiet seclusion. She imagined she was once again looking on as the half-grown child changed into a bright red fish before her eyes and darted with flashes of light through the water swirling so darkly or took on the form of a bird fluttering among shadowy branches. But into the midst of her dreamlike thoughts came bursting with rude force the abhorrent, bewildering emotions brought on by the present situation. With an involuntary sigh, she opened her eyes fully and looked out into the beauty of the dark. Before long, she noticed it was growing lighter across the wide water. The brightness was coming closer, the treetops catching its glow as it passed over them. Her growing unease told her that this was a being from the world to which she belonged but which she had for the past year lacked the resolution to claim as her own. It was not Keikobad, the Spirit King himself and the father of her mistress, who was approaching, or she would have been trembling even more intensely. As the terrace grew ever brighter, the aura of the spirit world penetrated to her very marrow. The messenger stood before her on the flat roof, clad in blue scale armor that sat snug on his compact frame. His blue-black hair was braided, and his eyes were glowing.

"Who are you?" asked the Nurse fearfully. "I have not seen you before."

"I am the Twelfth. And that should suffice for you," the messenger answered. "It is mine to ask questions and yours to answer. Is she bearing an unborn child in her womb? Has that vile state befallen her during this past month? Woe to you and me and all of us if it were so."

The Nurse answered with a vehement no.

"She therefore casts no shadow?" the messenger continued.

"None!" replied the Nurse. "I may give you the same assurance I gave the Eleven who came before you every time the moon had waned. She no more casts a shadow than if her body were made of rock crystal. It is even so that whatever she leaves behind her—stones, grass, or water—gleams more brightly, as if all those things were emeralds and topazes."

"Give thanks to your creator that it is so; give him thanks upon your knees, you heedless, blameworthy hag."

"Heedless? Blameworthy? Was I expected to grasp and hold a slippery fish in the water with my bare hands? Could I have held fast to a stubborn young gazelle by its horns? Why did he give her the power to transform herself? That was how she fell into the clutches of humankind! What was the good of my vigilance, my constant fear?"

"Each of us must be put to the test," replied the messenger.

"But then why," the Nurse retorted, "has she in turn lost a wondrous power which now could stand her in such good stead? She could have used it to slip loose from her doom in the same way she fell victim to it!"

"All these events are bound in time; they would not be tests if it were not so. Twelve moons have gone down, and three days are now coming!"

"Three days!" cried the Nurse with boundless joy.

The messenger cast her a stern glance. "Who taught you to measure moments of time against one another? Concentrate and watch over her with a hundred eyes. The Golden Water is on its wanderings, and it would not be good were she to chance upon it."

"The water of life?" cried the Nurse. "I have never seen it surge up, but I know it is full of mysterious powers. Could it help her to find a shadow?"

She would gladly have asked more questions, but she thought she heard a noise behind her, coming from the bed-chamber. She turned her head and in the soft light from the hanging lamp saw the Emperor, who had silently risen from his wife's side and was now standing fully dressed. The Nurse turned back quickly, but the messenger had vanished, and the brightness encircling him seemed to have dispersed through the surroundings. Treading lightly, the Emperor stepped over the body of the Nurse, who had prostrated herself and was lying with her face pressed to the ground. He paid her as little heed as if she were no more than a carpet lying there. He walked swiftly out to the edge of the roof and peered with head leaning forward into the faint break of day. From a considerable distance, the quickening air carried toward him what he was craving to hear. Noiselessly the grooms led his horse through the plane trees; he always commanded that its hoofs be tied with cloth, as it was his custom to ride out early to the hunt, before daybreak, leaving his wife while she still lay asleep, and not returning home until late, when the torches were already blazing on the landings of the stairs and the bedchamber was softly lit by the nine sconces of a hanging lamp. He had even so never neglected to pass even a single night of this past year, whose twelfth month had just now come to an end, by the side of his wife.

The Nurse had gone inside and set herself down at the edge of the bed, by the feet of the sleeping Empress, observing her ward with ambivalent affection. She took one of the torches from the lamp overhead and held it to the side: nary a shadow was to be seen on the wall, not from her head, her shoulders, her lovely slender hips. The sleeper began thrashing about, her face distorted in pain as a soft moan rose from her throat to her lips. Suddenly her eyes opened as she sat up in bed, as wide awake as a forest animal casting off sleep in an instant.

"He's gone away," she said, "and this time he'll be away for three nights."

The Nurse flinched as she thought of the messenger's words, but she regained control at once.

"What do you dream of when you sleep?" she hastily asked. "Your dreams must be bad."

"He has gone out into the mountains to look for his red falcon," said the Empress, "and he will not rest until he has found it, even if he has to remain away for thirty days and thirty nights."

"Alas that we have fallen into the hands of humankind," the Nurse answered. "Has it really gone so far that when you sleep you look almost exactly like their kind?"

"Why did you not let me go on sleeping?" cried the Empress. "How am I supposed to pass the tedious hours? If only I could follow him. Oh why did I have to lose the talisman?"

"Ill-fated child that you should have lost it! Did I not bind you by your very soul to protect it and hold it fast? Your fate depends on it, I said."

"I did not know then, to be sure, that it was the talisman giving me the power to slip out of my own shape and into that of any animal I chose. Now I know it, though, and must endure my punishment. How delightful my days would be if I still had it instead of being forced to watch the bleak, dreary days pass away between my nights of bliss. What a wondrous life I would have by day; how I would love to wind up in the arms of my lord and master in a different shape each day!"

"One time was enough," said the Nurse gloomily.

"Does that mean," the Empress replied with animation, "you believe he would have been able to take me captive so quickly if his red falcon hadn't flown at my head and blinded me with relentless blows from its wings that put out the fire in my eyes and forced me to come to ground in a thorn bush?"

"But how could he have thrown a spear at you, that murderer, that dull-eyed spawn of hell?"

"Did you expect him to recognize what I really was behind the shape I had taken on?" the Empress answered. "He has since sworn to me often enough that the look streaming out of the gazelle's eye made his arm grow unsteady and caused his spear merely to graze me along the neck instead of piercing my throat."

The Nurse growled out half a curse.

"I had just enough time not to give myself away with a glance, but to flit more quickly than I can tell it here, from the body of a gazelle into the one I inhabit now, and to raise my arms beseechingly to him. For he had leapt down from his horse and seized his remaining spear, arm drawn back to hurl it; his eyes were red from the speed and wildness of the chase, all his features tensed, so that before him—him whom I loved even at the very first glimpse and kept luring—I felt a terrifying fear of death and let out a piercing scream. It was this first scream, he told me, that awakened him from his frenzy and saved both our lives. Never before, though," she added in a low voice, "has any woman met with an abrupt change like the one that passed over his face—from the huntsman's deadly menace to the lover's gentle rapture. Alas, only that one time and never again did I so totally belong to him. Never again will I see his face undergo such a change."

She raised her eyes and continued: "He has vowed to me that no mortal could bear up more than once in a lifetime under a happiness bursting in so suddenly. It must be true, because I saw him striking out with mad rage after that very hour, when his red falcon flew into sight and he threw stones as he followed the bird, in his wild fury even hurling his dagger at it three times for having battered my eyes with its wings. I will never forget the long look the bleeding falcon, perched on a high rock, fixed on his master before it turned away and vanished, beating its wings in painful exhaustion."

The Nurse had stood up and gone out onto the flat roof; she knew only too well the whole story of that hunt and that first hour of love, as if it had been burned into her soul with a red-hot stylus. She cared as little about the fate of the red falcon as she did about the happiness of the lovers, the flames of whose passion kept blazing no less brightly after being reignited over and over for three hundred nights. Only one thought filled her; she could hardly wait to see the sun rise; she could not abide the faintness of dawn. All things must cast their shadows so that the only being that cast none might stand out from the rest all the more gloriously; she wanted to confirm for herself by a quick glance the condition bound up with a fearsome turn of fate, if only it could last for three more days. Filled with impatience, she looked up at the sky, already lightening to a greenish turquoise tinge; her keen eye at once caught sight of a bird slowly circling at a great height. It was not yet reflecting the sun's rays.

The Empress had now come out onto the roof, and the Nurse asked again: "What did you dream about before awakening?"

"About humans, I believe," answered the Empress.

"Disgusting," replied the Nurse. "I could read in your face that your dream was about something repulsive. Woe that we are here; woe to him who is the cause of it."

"Why are the faces of humankind so savage and ugly and those of beasts so fair and lovely?" said the Empress.

"She has a dread of him and all those like him," the Nurse muttered to herself. "She doesn't see him."

"If only I could once more turn into an otter and go streaming through the rapids," said the Empress. "Finding my way with no markers like a snake upon the ground or a hawk high in the air is pure delight, but love is more."

"Clinging to mortal men and women means pouring oneself into a vessel filled with holes," murmured the Nurse.

The Empress spotted the falcon circling high overhead,

and the Nurse watched with satisfaction the sunlight now reflected off its wings. It seemed to be descending slowly, though still gleaming in the light; its talons were sparkling like jewels, or else it was holding a jewel in its claws.

"Oh happy day," the Empress exclaimed suddenly. "It is the red falcon, my lord's favorite! It is healed of its wound; it has forgiven us."

The falcon hovered aloft with wings outspread.

"The talisman," cried the Empress in a loud voice. "The falcon has it and is bringing it back to me."

The Nurse hurried inside and came back with a green silken cloak glittering with pearls and precious stones. She held it high.

"See how we honor you and your gifts, you who are good," they called out, "you who are regal and magnanimous!"

The falcon soared high up and off to the side, on a gentle arc. With a single beat of its wings it then suddenly swooped downwards and something darted with a whooshing sound past the two women's faces; then in the twinkling of an eye the bird was once more high in the air and the talisman lay on the Empress's garment. The letters and characters engraved in the pale white stone glowed like fire or flashes from living eyes.

"I can read this writing," the Empress said, her color changing.

The Nurse cringed, because what was written there was unfathomable to her, as it had always been. A strange, conflicted thought ran through her mind; she quickly reached for the stone, wanting to tear it away and hide the writing, but it was too late. As fast as a lightning bolt the writing had been read and its meaning instantly grasped.

Her arm stiff, the Empress held the talisman out in front of her; it was as if she were looking through it into hell itself, and from her mouth came words not like one reading out her sentence but more dreadful yet, as if they were mounting, numb and frightful, from the breast of someone in a deep sleep:

"Curses and death to any mortal who undoes this binding; to stone will turn the hand of him who has loosed the tie, unless it avert that fate by obtaining a shadow from earth; to stone the body that hand belongs to; to stone the eye once aglow in that body—the senses remain alive on the inside so as to taste eternal death with the tongue of life—the time has been fixed by the cycles of the stars."

"It feels to me," said the Empress, letting her arm drop, "as though I had known this even in my cradle; perhaps my father whispered it into my ear as I slept; woe to me that I could have forgotten!"

The Nurse stayed as silent as the grave.

"Now I understand what I did not understand before," said the Empress as she hung the talisman on a strand of pearls between her breasts. But her eyes, though wide open, knew nothing of what her hands were doing, as if she were sleepwalking.

"That shadow is my shadow, the one I do not cast. I heard my lord speaking about something like this to one of his trusted friends: he said, 'I do not wish to sit in judgment on my own or pronounce a sentence of death before I have repaid the earth with my own life.' It is through casting a shadow that humans recompense the earth for their existence. I did not know how much this dark thing means to them. A curse upon me that I heard all this with such unconcern, as if it had nothing to do with me! I will be his death because I walk the earth but do not cast a shadow!"

Her initial numbness gave way to deathly fear. She was gripped with unspeakable yearning to rescue her beloved. She seized hold of the Nurse and held her fast; to the Empress it seemed as if help and salvation could come only from this one ally, this friend to whom since her girlhood she had so often gone running with her fears and her needs.

"You have never failed me," she cried and wrapped her arms tightly around the old one's form; "help me now, you who alone can do so. You forgave me everything; you trudged after me when I left our island; you clambered over the Mountains of the Moon; for three months you wandered through cities and hamlets until you found out by ceaseless inquiry where I had alighted; you lived among mortals, the mere sight of whom set you shuddering; you ate with them and slept by their side; you let their breath waft over you: and all that for my sake. Help me now; nothing is hidden from you; you find ways and trace out means; all terms and conditions are open to your sight; and you know how to evade forbidden actions! Help me gain a shadow, you who alone know how to! Show me where to find one, even if it means flinging aside my garment and plummeting into the depths of the sea. Tell me the secret of where I may buy one, even if it means giving away every treasure that the open-handedness of my beloved has heaped upon me, nay even if it were at the cost of half the blood in my veins!"

The Nurse's silence alarmed her even more, and she tried looking into the old one's eyes. Just at that moment the first of the sun's beams blazed out toward them like torches. The terrible cunning and unyielding rigidity of the Nurse's face pierced the Empress deeply, and she felt abandoned as never before in her life. The confidante who had guided her from childhood on had now pulled away. The Empress was alone. But she was one of those whose power increases with opposition.

"You know, you evil old creature," she cried, "and you have known all along; you have seen it approaching and were filled with joy; you know the day and the hour that will bring my death, and you are jubilant in counting down the days as if a great festival were drawing near. And a festival is indeed what you consider it, a day that when it dawns will bring you reward or leniency; my father will realize what price he has paid to buy a cowardly, treacherous heart. You have made a grave mistake, however; you were hoping to deliver me over to my doom all unawares, but a bird came down from the sky and gave me warning. I am vigilant, fully conscious of the power conferred on me over you. I do not wish to know when disaster will strike, even though it be this very hour. It might paralyze me if I knew. I ask you no questions; I command you instead to obtain a shadow for me, even if you have to lose your life in the attempt and I along with you, even if we both have to turn to stone while our hearts go on beating. My father is far distant, but I am near you. Let us now set off, you ahead of me, I behind you, and see to it by the power of the Mighty Names that I procure a shadow! From here and nowhere else we start out on our way, today and not tomorrow, at this very hour, not when the sun is standing higher."

The nurse trembled and did not know what reply she might give. Everything she had plotted in her shrewdness, everything that had shaped itself with near certainty into her day of deliverance was now no more than a blur before her eyes. It was almost with hatred that she had looked at her mistress as she slept, twitching slightly and resembling an earthly woman. But now the ruler with absolute sovereignty was again standing before her, and the old one felt suffusing her from head to foot the obligation to serve. She began indistinctly murmuring vague reassurances.

"Not a word," ordered the Empress, "unless it be to point us the way, no subterfuges or excuses to avoid what I command. And no hesitation, for you know that every second burns into my heart."

"Child, if I but knew the way even now and could perhaps come to learn the circumstances under which a shadow might be obtained . . . "

"But we must set out," cried the young woman, "to our goal! You ahead, with me behind, before we draw another breath."

"Obtain is not the right word, either," the Nurse muttered. "To cajole one instead from its rightful owner through servility or trickery."

"Lead on to where such a one dwells, even if it were to a dragon with its spawn."

"To something even worse, perhaps; are you not gripped by an uneasy feeling?"

"Lead on, you devious one, you speaker with forked tongue," cried the Empress in a rage, hauling the Nurse to her feet. "You're worse than a dragon yourself."

"What is worse than a dragon, more disgusting to the sight and repulsive to the soul," said the Nurse, casting a hard look onto the young woman's face, "is humankind."

"Take me to that person whose shadow is for sale, that I may buy it, and I will kiss his feet."

"Mad, foolish child," cried the Nurse, "do you know what you're saying? Don't you cringe with loathing before humans, even deep into your dreams, though you know so little about them? And now you want to dwell with them! Trade and deal with them? Talk after talk, breath after breath? Look at their faces? Nuzzle into their meanness? Flatter their baseness? Be their handmaid? Because that's what you would be reduced to. Doesn't it horrify you?"

"I want a shadow," cried the Empress, "so let us go down so that I may serve one of their kind for the shadow. Where is the house? Take me there! That is my will!"

"The house?" replied the Nurse, as her expression grew dim. "If I knew where it stands we would be closer to our goal than we are. We must find it."

The younger woman hung on the words of the old one; she realized that what the Nurse had just spoken was the truth, and her pallor grew yet more severe.

"You know neither the person nor the house," she whispered, "so it means both of us must seek and both of us find, you before me, I behind." Her firm resolve blazed up inside her like a flame in an alabaster vessel.

"I know that everything is for sale with them, but that is all I know," said the Nurse. "Off we go now, and write a letter to your beloved."

"What should I write?" asked the Empress, as obedient as a child.

The shrewd old one gave her advice about how to phrase the letter. It would be necessary to treat her absence from the blue palace with prudence, but nothing was to be said about what the Empress feared and even less about what she was proposing to do. She held the sheet made of smooth swan parchment delicately in the flat of her left hand as she drew the marks with her right, but her hand grew heavy, and sigh upon sigh was forced from her. However harmless she made the words she set down, with however much beauty she arranged them, it seemed that a proclamation of disaster kept forcing its way into the text. Everything seemed to carry a double meaning, the beauty of the marks and signs itself became fearsome, and she brought the letter to a close with many sighs; a crystal tear fell onto the parchment. The Nurse looked on all the while and could not understand what was so hard. She took the letter from the Empress's hand, rolled and folded it together, enveloped it in a cloth embroidered with pearls, and slid it into a flat case made of gilded leather. The Empress wove her own hair ribbon through the golden loops on the case and tied it into a knot that only the Emperor would know how to undo. The letter was now sealed and handed over to a messenger, a skilled horseman who knew the roads well.

Chapter Two

While the Emperor was riding along at a brisk trot to overtake the hunting party, the Nurse, moving ahead of the Empress, kept a downward course, coming to a halt in the most densely populated city of the Southeastern Islands. Their attire was shabby, the Nurse in a garment of black and white scraps that made her look like a spotted snake, the Empress looking even plainer, her dazzling face obscured after being smeared with a dark liquid. No one paid them any attention as they strode quickly along the area that bordered the river flowing through the large city. The yellowish water bore large patches of dark colors constantly being discharged anew from the dyers' quarter above the bridge; the sharp odor of tanning bark penetrated their noses from the opposite bank, where the squat houses of the tanners and dyers stood, and animal hides were stretched out to dry on small wooden poles along the sloping bank of the river. On this side lived the blacksmiths and nail makers, and the air was filled with the din of pounding hammers from the glare of open fires and from the stench of singed hooves. The Nurse made her way quickly and confidently, as if she were following a familiar path, while the Empress followed behind her. They came out onto a bridge across which a large multitude was jostling—porters, soldiers, two-wheeled carts, and mounted riders. The Nurse pushed through the crowd, the Empress trying to stay close behind her, though she was unable to. Seeing human faces this close, everything appalling about their features assailed her as never before. She tried to be courageous in passing them by at close range; though her feet could, her heart could not. Every hand that moved seemed to be grabbing at her, and all those mouths were hideous so close up. The pitiless, ravenous looks—but also frightened, she seemed to realize—on so many faces all swarmed together in her bosom. She made an effort to stay close when she saw the Nurse looking back toward her but was so strongly jostled she almost fell; suddenly she was nearly under the hooves of a large mule, when she caught sight of the animal's gentle, knowing eyes and rallied. The mule's rider struck it over the head with a club, because it had stopped so as not to trample the shaking woman.

"Has it reached a point where I must change myself into a beast and deliver myself over to the cruel hands of men?" This was what went through her spirit, and she trembled, forgetting herself for a moment and finding herself at the end of the bridge, she knew not how, shoved along by the crowd. She saw the Nurse standing by a food stand, an open stall, waiting for her. Lying there were some lovely small fish, rose-gold in color, with a black man rooting around among them. A skinned lamb, its head looking down, was hanging from a beam and looking at her with gentle eyes. An arm reached out and drew her in; it was the Nurse, who had observed the Empress turn pale and close her eyes briefly and who pulled her out of the crush and into a narrow side street. Here there were fewer passers-by, and those few were laden with bundles of cloth. Here and there large swathes of dyed cloth were hanging down from the houses on drying poles. Half-grown children were lugging vats and dark-colored material for soaking. The Nurse had come to a stop in front of a low-roofed dwelling among the dyers' houses and was listening as the voices of people quarreling inside made their way outdoors. The shouts of several indignant men could be heard, answered with rancor and arrogance by a woman who sounded still young; then another man's voice chimed in; it had a deep, unruffled timbre that appeared to be urging the others to calm down. But the young woman raised her voice even more rancorously and arrogantly than before.

"I like the sound of her voice," said the Nurse, signaling to the Empress to press herself close to the wall.

The bickering inside grew more vehement, until finally the deep voice, the one that had had the least to say, now spoke in a forceful tone with great emphasis but total composure. Just after that, the other men's voices, disgruntled and jarring, came closer to the front door. The Nurse pretended to be moving along, though as slowly as if she were old and sick and were able to hobble only slightly with each step. The Empress was creeping along beside her. Three men stepped out of the house, one with one eye, one with one arm, and the third, much younger, was hunchbacked and hobbled because of a paralytic hip.

"In truth, my brothers," the one-eyed man said, "the varlet who put my eye out twenty-two years hence has not harmed me as much as our brother's wife harms our brother."

"You speak true," said the one-armed man, as they made their way along the lane, "and the accursed millworks that tore off my arm fifteen years gone did not damage me as much as she does him."

"And the camel that stepped on my back and broke it full nine years ago did not injure me so gravely!" added the youngest.

"Verily the arrogance and spitefulness of this woman, our sister-in-law," the oldest spoke again, "make her an evil as dire as the plague, and that is why she has remained unfruitful even though she is young and beautiful and our brother is a man among men."

"This is the dwelling we want," said the Nurse, turning her face away from the three brothers and toward the dyer's house. She quickly stepped inside, passing through the entry and into a low shed so old it was close to tumbling down as she pulled the Empress along behind her.

"We have to wait until the man is out of the house," she whispered, pointing to a gap in the wall at which she had placed her eye. She pointed out another gap to the Empress, and they both peered into the only room the house contained. The Empress saw a young woman very shabbily dressed, her face beautiful but sullen as she sat on the floor staring into empty air with her jaws clenched; she also saw a tall, sturdy man about forty years old balancing an enormous bale of scarlet cloth with his dark-blue hands and tying it with cords so he could load it onto his back, which was as strong as a camel's: this was Barak the Dyer. As he worked he would now and then turn his face toward the wall, showing a low forehead, protruding ears, and a gaping mouth. To the Empress he seemed repulsively ugly, and she judged the young woman to be mean and nasty. It was easy to notice that the Dyer would have liked to speak to his wife; when he had tied up the bundle, he paced clumsily back and forth on his big feet, made as if to lift up something that lay on the floor not far from her, soiled his hands in a puddle of run-off dyeing water while murmuring a few words and looking sideways at his wife. Her glance kept doggedly sweeping past him and into empty space the whole time, though, as if he were not there. Finally he sighed, hoisted the heavy burden onto his back with a single heave, and went out the door bent down like a beast of burden, but with firm, even steps. The woman stood up as soon as she found herself alone. She went through the room sluggishly and with her dragging feet kicked over an old stone mortar; the liquid spilled out onto the stained floor. She bent halfway over to wipe it up but twisted her lips into a sneer and let it just lie there. She went to the place where she and the Dyer slept; low to the ground, it was in the farthest corner of the brick wall and covered with a few pillows and blankets. She made the bed by kicking into place anything that needed straightening. Then she walked away and from the middle of the room cast a fierce glance back toward the bed. With a yawn she went to a niche in the wall and fetched out a meagre supply of yellow-green olive branches; she flung the wood down onto the fireplace, which was nothing more than a smoke-blackened opening in the wall and then slowly stood back up like someone tired out from long hours of work. She stroked the sides of her body in a downward motion, and when she felt how slender her hips were, she smiled instinctively.

"This is the place for us," the Nurse whispered, "we'll go inside," as they left the shed and stepped all the way through the door of the dwelling place.

The Empress had never set foot across the threshold of any human abode except for her own palace; she was seized with nameless apprehension that again made her close her eyes as she felt herself reeling, so much so that she almost tripped over the long handle of a ladle on the floor. She made to support herself by reaching for a cauldron that hung from a chain; it tipped and spattered her with a bright scarlet liquid. When the wife saw hastily crossing her threshold—at which a strange face rarely appeared—an old crone who looked like a speckled magpie and a young woman who stumbled—she was forced to laugh out loud and couldn't stop for a long time. Meanwhile, the Nurse understood how to turn the whole situation deftly to her own purpose through an immediate flood of words by way of introduction.

It was no wonder, she said, that her daughter had tripped, though she wouldn't fail to ask pardon for doing so, but the girl wasn't used to being in a city and had grown weary from traipsing along highways and byways, from asking questions and searching; several people had sent her in the wrong direction, perhaps from ignorance, perhaps from spite, but the daughter wouldn't give up until she found the right house, and now that she saw with her own eyes the exquisite beauty of her young mistress—here the Nurse bowed down to the Dyer's Wife, touching the ground with her forehead and bidding her daughter to do likewise—there could no longer exist the slightest doubt in her mind that she had reached the right place.

What did she mean, the right place? Who had sent them? And for what reason? What was all this supposed to mean? asked the Dyer's Wife, keyed up with astonishment.

When the Nurse asserted with further kowtowing that she was well aware of the young mistress's need for servants and thus was now humbly entreating permission—at this point kissing the seam of the Wife's garment—to have put to the test her seasoned proficiency, garnered over years, robust though she still was, and the proficiency of her daughter, the young woman couldn't help going into gales of laughter, especially because both strangers had a dark blue spot in the middle of their foreheads from contact with the dirty floor. As to who it was who had guided them to this house and pointed out exactly where they were to take up service, the Nurse delivered a profusion of words, none of them very clear. What finally emerged was that it was someone they had met by chance on a bridge, not the new bridge, but a different one; a young man, practically still a boy, quite slim and graceful. Perhaps he'd only been acting on behalf of the other man, somewhat older, proud and courtly, who looked like a prince and had at first held himself slightly off to the side but had ended up speaking with her; yes, she believed when she thought about it that it could be none other than he; it was clear that their young mistress had in him a truly well-meaning admirer and patron. Here she gave such a strange and significant wink of her red-rimmed eye that the Dyer's Wife shrank back a step and declared to herself with a sweet shudder of amazement that she must indeed have such a well-wisher somewhere out there in the world, even though she might never have seen him or received any sign of life from him up to now. The Nurse was right by her side again in a flash, and precisely because she could sense that the woman was not turning away from her but toward her instead, and on the deepest inner level at that, she affected to fear the opposite and called on God as her witness that there could never be a more dreadful misunderstanding than if she had in fact come to the wrong place! Now she hardly trusted herself to ask if the further points of evidence tallied: if this exquisitely beautiful young lady before them was indeed married, married for two full years but so far childless, oddly enough—yes, that described her—and married to a man, a dyer by trade, of more mature years—he could easily be his wife's father—ungainly, with a gaping mouth and large ears? Well, true enough, that was more or less the way her husband Barak was built. And was it true that were there three unmarried brothers-in-law at home, nasty, burdensome fellows, one-armed, one-eyed, and humpbacked, quarrelsome idlers and freeloaders at their brother's table, incurring the deadly hatred of her secret admirer because of the harassment they were constantly causing the beautiful woman of his dreams? From this moment on, nothing was more indisputable in the mind of the beautiful Dyer's Wife than that she enjoyed the favor of a hidden friend whose thoughts and feelings were wondrously tender. What struck her as most enchanting of all was that here was someone who knew every detail about her, watched over her and shared in all the afflictions and insults of which her young life was allegedly so full; these thoughts all of a sudden flooded the dreariness of her everyday life with so much light that its reflection shone out in her face.

"What good fortune for us," the Nurse now exclaimed, "that we have indeed stopped at the right dwelling! You are truly the chosen one, that rare beauty, select among thousands, the one of whom I know something which in knowing warms and rejoices the heart within me. You are she who has raised herself on high by renouncing her husband's incessant but vain demands for endearment and has said to herself: 'I am glutted with motherhood before I ever even tasted it.' You are she who has chosen the slenderness of an undamaged body and in her wisdom abjured a ravaged womb and withered, sagging breasts." The old one spoke these words in a loud voice and a kind of solemn descant, and the grotesque features she had assumed for the world of humans really did resemble the head of a spotted snake. The Dyer's Wife kept looking at her toothless mouth and the thin lips through which her glib-speaking tongue was darting quickly, but could not tell what was taking place inside her; something like her present feeling had been lodged deep within, darkly, between sleep and waking, throughout the two years of her unfruitful marriage. She had never said anything about it out loud, not even to herself, although it might perhaps have crept past her lips unspoken as she lay half-asleep, responding sullenly and lethargically, like an unwilling child, to the inexhaustible gentleness of the strong Dyer. The feeling remained unspoken, and no one but Barak could ever sense it, but even though no more than an inkling of it had penetrated to the depths of his soul, his thick tongue never said anything about it; now this stranger, this old woman, however, was singing it all into her ears so that it sounded like an accolade mingled with prophecies and linked to some alluring account of an unknown suitor. No one, man or woman, had ever spoken to her like this. Embarrassed but charged with a sense of her own importance as well, she ran hot and cold; curiosity and shame tore her away from herself and toward the old woman; she could feel her excitement causing tears to rise in her throat, and she pursed her mouth as she turned away to prevent them from breaking out. Behind her back the Nurse was secretly signaling to the Empress by blinking her repugnant, lidless eyes and pointing to the faint shadow the Dyer's Wife was casting in the half-dark room; she made as if she were stroking the shadow, her fingers spread out toward it as if she could pull it up off the floor and fix it to her mistress's body. Then she crept around to face the Dyer's Wife and through further gestures of deference began fanning the fire of confusion she had already kindled.

"Mistress dear, take pity on us and deign to take us on as your eager servants! If only we knew how to attain your esteemed favor so that you might put us to the test here and then take us with you later on into your life of bliss!"

"Foolish one," said the Wife, "here and nowhere else am I passing my life of bliss. The ladles must be cleaned, the stirring poles scraped and scrubbed, mortars and pestles scoured, vats and buckets emptied, the floor washed, the water trough filled, the cold kettle stoked with kindling and the hot one stirred, the animal skin scraped, and the sack of wheat ground in the hand mill; oil must be fetched from the vessel and fish put into the pan; the fish must be fried and the oil cakes baked. Barak, my husband, is hungry, and his one-eyed, one-armed, and hunchbacked brothers are all expecting to be fed too."

"Come closer, my daughter," cried the old one as if in a frenzy, "come closer and lift your hands. We must put ourselves to the proof before our mistress so that she will admit us into her radiant glory!"

"What foolish talk is this?" the woman asked with a laugh.

"Hither ye pans and flare forth fire!" cried the Nurse in a piercing voice, not answering the Dyer's Wife. The cooking pans flew through the air into her hands, and the green oil branches began crackling.

"Who are you?" the Dyer's Wife asked, her voice shaking, "and who is the young woman? Is this silent one really your daughter? She doesn't look like you. Why is she skulking in the dark and staring at me so?"

The fire flared up and caused the Wife's shadow to fall across the dirt floor onto the wall opposite.

"Hither ye fish from fishes' barrel!" cried the old woman as her hands constantly busied themselves over the fire. Seven

fish flew through the air and past the old woman's scrawny
fingers, their golden-pink bodies lining up side by side on the
chopping block.

"Who are you?" the woman asked again as she gasped for
breath.

"Herbs from my mistress's herb garden!" the old woman
called out as a command, thrusting her claws into the empty
air, from which they were filled with herbs whose fragrance
pervaded the room.

"What mistress?" cried the young woman as if in a dream,
half mad with curiosity and fear.

The old one tossed the fish into the pan, poured oil over
them, and set them on the fire. "Ask your mirror!" she replied
over her shoulder.

"I have no mirror," the Dyer's Wife answered quickly. "I
arrange my hair over the water trough."

The fire flared up higher; the shadow surged up too, growing more and more beautiful.

"Where will this end?" the Empress wondered, trembling
with anxiety at the strangeness of it all. It seemed to her that
the fish in the pan were calling out together in a lamenting
tone. Indeed, they were crying out very clearly the following
words, as if intoning them:

> Mother, mother, let us come home;
> The door is barred tight, we can find no way in.

"Where am I?" the Empress asked. "Am I the only one
hearing this?"

The words penetrated to a deeper and more secret place
inside her than anything had ever pierced. The Nurse was

frantically busy by the fire; the pans leapt up, the oil sizzled, the fish crackled, the wheat cakes puffed up. She called some words out into the air and in her outstretched hand flashed an exquisite ribbon woven through with pearls and precious stones, like the one with which the Empress had sealed her letter. In her other hand was a round mirror. She knelt down in front of the Dyer's Wife, who was squatting on the ground before her. The Nurse guided the young woman's hand, weaving the ribbon into her hair; the Wife's face was glowing in the round mirror as if reborn in a cleansing fire. The fish sang piteously:

> We dwell in darkness and in fear;
> Mother, let us enter in
> Or call upon our father dear
> That he may open up the door!

"Do they not hear that?" the Empress thought. It grew dark before her eyes, but she did not lose her senses. She could see the other two women clearly. The young one was hunched over, looking fixedly into the mirror, as the older one kept passing between her and the stove.

"I've had dreams like this," came from the lips of the Dyer's Wife.

Her face looked strangely different, and her next words could not be understood. The old woman bounded to her side like a lover, knelt down beside her, and whispered directly into her ear: "Did you also dream that it would be this way forever?"

Their exchange was in broken syllables. The young woman caved in for sheer happiness as her eyes rolled up and showed only their gleaming whites.

"Three nights to start with—can you be strong?" hissed the Nurse. "Three nights without your husband."

The Wife nodded three times. "That's nothing—but what then?" she whispered. "Is what I have to do something bad? Is it something terrible? What is it going to be like?"

"Oh you innocent child," cried the Nurse as she stroked the other one's hands, cheeks, and feet. "It is nothing at all."

"Will you stand by my side and aid me?" the Dyer's Wife asked in a murmur.

"Are we not your slaves as of this very hour?" cried the Nurse.

"But tell me what it will be like," the young woman asked.

"You are expecting great things but will marvel at small ones," the Nurse replied. "Those three nights and your firm resolve—they are what will test you."

"My resolve is taken and the three nights are easy for me; tell me how the task will be fulfilled!"

"You creep out of the house between day and night and make for flowing water," the Nurse said.

"The river is nearby," the young woman replied.

"You turn your back to the flowing water and take off your clothes, keeping nothing on but the slipper on your left foot."

"Nothing but that?" said the Dyer's Wife, smiling fearfully.

"Then you take seven fish like the ones there, toss them over your right shoulder with your left hand into the water and say three times: 'Depart from me, accursed ones, and dwell within my shadow.' Then you are forever free of the undesired ones and will enter into the splendor of which this ribbon and the meal I have prepared here are but a feeble foretaste."

"What does it mean when I say to those who are undesired, 'Dwell within my shadow'?"

"It is part of the pact you will make, and it means your shadow will fall away from you in that hour, whereupon you will be as radiant in front as you are in back."

The woman glanced past the mirror with a lost look. "I shall do it," she then said.

"Mother, woe is us!" the fish cried out, their voices dying as they were fully cooked.

Only the Empress heard their cry and it pierced through her; she had to close her eyes for a goodly time. When she opened them again, she saw by the glow of the dying fire how the young woman was leaning forward, trying to kiss the Nurse's hand. Near the front of the room, by the fireplace, a sleeping place for Barak the Dyer had been arranged from one half of the marital bed; to the rear, a curtain had been drawn before the wife's half. The Nurse bowed low before the Dyer's Wife and drew her daughter behind her toward the door.

"What happened?" asked the Empress as they drifted through the night

"Much," replied the Nurse.

"Is it finished?" the Empress asked, touching the Nurse in a confiding way; now that they were no longer among humans she was no longer filled with dread.

The old woman fixed her with an almost scornful look.

"Patience!" she said. "All in good time."

CHAPTER THREE

Barack the Dyer came home late. He found the dwelling dark but suffused with lush fragrances like the house of a rich man. After striking a light he saw in complete amazement the marital bed split in two, one half seemingly set up for him in a totally unwonted spot near the hearth, the other with a piece of cloth draped in front of it. He went over to the curtain, and after covering the light with his hand he saw his wife sleeping like a child, her fists balled up. She was breathing gently, and he felt how desirable she was, but he kept himself in check, went over to the hearth with quiet footsteps and, by following the scent, found the remains of a delectable meal of fish and oil cakes seasoned with herbs the like of which he had never eaten. He saved half a fish and a portion of cake and with quiet footsteps carried these leftovers out to the shed so that the younger of his brothers, the hunchbacked one, would find them during the night or early in the morning, when he was craving something to eat. Then he went to his sleeping place and said a short prayer while sitting on the bed; afterwards he stayed there for some time not moving and looking intently over to the curtain that blocked him from seeing his wife. There was no movement behind it, however, and with a soft sigh—but powerful, like everything else about him—he stretched out his limbs and fell asleep at once. The next morning he went out to the river before sunrise, taking a full-sized pounding mortar and working with it outside there, a hundred paces from the house, so as not to cut short his wife's sleep. When he returned he saw two strange women creeping past the threshold of his dwelling as if they were at home here.

"These are kinswomen of mine, come to serve me of their own free will," said the Wife; he was surprised at her being up this early.

When the two women bent down to kiss the hem of her dress, her bearing was so graceful as they went about it that he thought he had never seen her so beautiful. But he had no time to feast his eyes on her. He hoisted a heavy stack of newly tanned animal skins onto his back; the old woman hurried over and lent him a hand. She preceded him to the door, opened it, and bowed when he passed her.

"Come back home soon, master" she said, "for my mistress is consumed with longing when you are not here." Then she was at her young mistress's side in a flash and showed her a face silently ridiculing the man on his way out.

"These moments are flowing gold dust," she hissed, "come here so that I may adorn you and take you away from here."

"There is nothing to concern us outside the house," said the woman.

"Then vouchsafe that I call hither him who is yearning to come."

"Who is it you mean?" the woman asked coldly, staring her firmly in the face.

The Nurse was dismayed but did not show it. "The man on the bridge," she retorted confidently, "it is he of whom I am speaking, the most wretched of all men! Only vouchsafe that I call on him and bring him hither, to the very threshold of longing and acceptance!"

"I want this house cleaned," said the Dyer's Wife, looking past the old woman. "The cauldrons must be gleaming and the mortars scoured, the stirring poles need to look like new, the floor cleaned, and all else put in order, one task at a time."

"But only consider, O my mistress," cried the Nurse in a pitiful voice, "that there is one whose knees tremble at the very thought of your loosened hair."

"The vats must be taken outside to soak, you shameless creature" answered the Dyer's Wife, "the troughs and vessels tended to, new kindling and firewood brought from the shed, five cords stacked high, fire lit under the cauldrons, the mills set to grinding, sparks set flying, beds made—go to it, right now! Get on with it, both of you! Barak, my husband, will be happy that I have two serving women."

"Woe to us," cried the old one, falling at the Wife's feet. "Let us depart from hence, my daughter; we are contemptible in the sight of our mistress, who does not desire that we should render her our true service!"

"Have you decided willingly to serve me or not?" shouted the Dyer's Wife spitefully, drawing her foot back so that the Nurse stumbled. "Have you pledged yourselves to me or not?" She stamped her feet.

The Nurse and the Empress went scurrying; they swiftly made the beds, took the vats and troughs outside for soaking, then quickly hauled firewood from the shed and stacked it, polished the mortars and grinders till they gleamed, and scrubbed clean the scoops and ladles. The Dyer's Wife had meanwhile taken the precious hair ribbon out from under her pillow and fetched the mirror. She sat on a bundle of dried herbs on the ground and preened herself, but her face was morose.

"You think you have me in your pockets," she called over her shoulder, "but you're not as shrewd as you think! So just fetch and carry now till you sweat."

"You must be hungry, mistress," said the old woman meekly. "Nothing makes a person so hungry as watching others work," she added, handing her a platter on which stood a variety of small pastry shells fragrant with delicate spices; the Dyer's Wife had never set her eyes on anything like them. She looked at the platter in amazement, then took it and ate one of the small savories after another. When Barak returned home at midday, the Wife wasn't hungry and left the meal untouched that the Nurse had cooked and that Barak relished. She also had very little to say and did not answer any of her husband's questions. With almost every bite he took, he turned his round eyes toward his wife; their whites were easy to see whenever he was on the alert or worried.

"Pray, you women eating with us," Barak said to the Empress and the Nurse, sitting some distance away and eating what was left, "pray that she may be able to eat again and that she may thrive. You should know," he continued, "that a week ago I summoned all my kinswomen to the house, and those goodwives spoke strong invocations over my wife here; and I must tell you that I ate seven times before nightfall of that which they had hallowed with blessings for fruitfulness. And though my wife be strange and different from others, yet I praise her strangeness and bow to the ground before her transformation, for happiness has come upon me and expectation fills my heart."

The young woman's face suddenly looked sallow and spiteful. "But what I must say to you," she said, her mouth twisted, "is that no bleary-eyed hags will have any say over my body and that whatever this man ate before nightfall has no power over my womanhood."

She stood up from the ground all of a sudden, went over

to her bed, and drew the curtain. Barak stood up as well and opened his mouth as if he wanted to speak, while his round eye stayed fixed on the curtain concealing his wife from him. He silently began the task of stacking an immense heap of dyed fabric and loading it onto his back. When he was finished, he went to the door, where he settled his burden more firmly on his powerful back. Then he said to the kinswomen with a friendly look, "I have no hard feelings toward my wife for her way of speaking, for I am joyful of heart, I want you to know, and I await the blessed ones who will come."

"There will come none," the wife whispered to herself, "not a one into this house; instead, there are those will leave it." She whispered it almost silently, remaining behind the curtain, so that no one could hear; but the Nurse heard it anyway, and her lashless eyes twitched.

The Dyer's Wife sat on her bed for a full hour without moving. After a long time the Nurse walked over to the curtain and whispered something toward the bed, but there came no answer.

"Alas," sighed the Empress, "living with men and women is more distressing than merely picturing them. Tell me, what is the strife between the spiteful woman and her coarse, ugly husband about?"

"About your shadow," answered the Nurse just as quietly.

The Wife suddenly stepped forward. "Why doesn't he come, you lying creature? Where is he whom you're forever talking about?" she asked sharply, turning dark red the second she had spoken. "You don't have to keep on repeating your story," she continued, "for I know he must be old and repulsive, and from that I can tell he sent you here before him as his bawd."

The Nurse said not a word.

"Just admit to me," the Dyer's Wife cried, "that you're being paid to pander and to delude me; tell me this is all trickery you're practicing to bewilder me!"

Still the Nurse remained silent.

"My slipper across your face, witch," the woman screamed, "take that for making me feel now for the first time how wretchedly miserable I am; take that"—and she struck the Nurse again—"for wanting to make my bad situation worse. Who is it that would have sent a creature like you into my house? Did he see me on the street and now dares to lust after me just like that? Answer me before I drive you off, and then ask him who gave him permission to cast his eye on me! Tell him that Barak is the strongest of all the dyers and has no equal among the laborers."

The Nurse remained motionless and persisted in her silence, only raising her head slightly off the ground, but it appeared as if she could not summon up the courage to meet the glance of her infuriated mistress. Only when the woman stopped berating her and began moving away with shuffling footsteps did the Nurse follow her with her eyes and whisper into empty space, as if to herself, "Look upon her, my lord. Does she not have the gliding gait of a thirsting gazelle?"

"My hands around your throat," shrieked the Dyer's Wife, who had heard every word and now spun on her heel, "to whom are you speaking, you witch?" The red had drained out of her face; now she turned pale and looked like a frightened child.

"To him who is standing outside, to him who has his hands outstretched toward your house, who has torn his garments for sheer longing and keen desire."

"Come here to me," said the Dyer's Wife in a changed voice, "come close but do not touch me." She sat down on her bed and let the Nurse come close. "You are a procuress," she said, "all the worse for me, and an ordinary one at that, and now you've come to me because I'm poor, trying your usual tricks on me, taking a chance I'll fall for them. I forgive you for that, but now it's time to leave me in peace and take this other one with you, for I don't want you to stay in my house any longer; all of this is what I was turning over in my mind while I was sitting on my bed not saying anything. I do not want to go anywhere with you, and I do not want to see the man who sent you, because I have wearied of him before even seeing him. The greedy and the lustful ones of this world are all alike, and their lusts are sickening to me."

She looked around the room as if she were pondering something.

"Many things here were filthy, and you have washed away the filth," she continued, "but that hasn't made anything better; I don't care for the gear and goods any more than I did before, and the house is gloomier than a prison. You came to me in an evil hour and whispered into my ear tales about the joys life has in store for me. That was your blackest lie; there is ahead of me nothing other than what has been. I am like a goat tethered to a stake; I can bleat night and day, but no one will pay attention. When I'm driven by hunger I take sustenance, and this is how I live from one day to another, and that is how it will go on for me, pathetic woman, until I have wrinkled cheeks and runny eyes like you."

Her words were overcome by tears, and she slumped forward. The old one supported her. Whole streams were pouring down her cheeks, and the Nurse took delight in watching her cry. She let the weeping young woman slide down onto the bed, stroking her cheeks and kissing the tips of her fingers and her knees.

"Oh you rarest and most exquisite of women, you are like incense that preserves its fragrance in cool air, you who are so severe against your own self."

"But why do you want to set that incense burning? That is not what I wish," the woman said in a weak voice and raised herself halfway up in the Nurse's arms.

"We are not speaking of ambergris here, nor of nard, but of yearning and fulfillment instead."

"Do not utter magic words," the young woman cried fearfully, cringing in the arms that were holding her tight and easing her back down onto the bed.

"Be at ease, unutterably lovely one, you yourself are the incense; your breath is more sweet-smelling than nard, and your glances stoke longing with the fire of rapture."

The Dyer's Wife struggled to get free of the Nurse's embrace but was still clinging to her at the same time; in a whirlwind of lechery and fear she could see into a shimmering weft of fire over their heads, out of which something was trying to take form and emerge. Her senses began to reel, and she had to close her eyes.

"Oh my master, can you resist her eyes when their light fades?" the Nurse whispered, close by the young woman's head. She looked up as she whispered these words.

"Who is that? There's no one there," the Dyer's Wife said breathlessly. She could feel her willpower draining away as she clung to the old woman's arm. "Whom are you speaking to?"

"To one who is nigh and aflame for you, to one who is calling to me: 'Cover her eyes, then, and when you open them for her once more, it will be my face looking down upon her feet.'"

"My eyes," said the woman, tearing herself away, "not for anything!"

"But you must do it," cried the Nurse in a cajoling voice. "Lie back down on your bed, all the way now, and let me spread this cloak over you, while my daughter covers your feet and gently lays her hand on your eyes—you've already granted permission, my mistress!"

"This must not come about," the Empress said to herself. "She does not want it! It must never come about," she repeated, even as the woman's eyes were pressing against the backs of her hands.

It had already come about simply by her saying those words. In the middle of the room was a living being resembling a man, one who had not been there before. She noticed him only out of the corner of her eye; his presence was powerful but furtive like that of a beast. The Empress could not bear having this apparition at her back. She stepped back and took her hands away from the eyes of the Dyer's Wife, who sat up and began shaking from fear and embarrassment. The Nurse bowed low to the ground before this new arrival, and he slowly turned his steps toward the beautiful Dyer's Wife. The Empress stepped behind her; she saw that one of his eyes was larger than the other and was throwing out a glance of strong brute ferocity. She then recognized that he was an ifrit, a demon that could assume any shape it chose so as to entice and dupe humans. She noticed how handsome he was, but the unrestrained rapacity spread over his features made his face appear more hideous to her than that of any human being she had encountered here on earth. She knew that ifrits lie in wait near the realm of the living, but never had one dared come so close to her. She trembled from head to foot with hatred and contempt as she rose to her full height, eyes blazing with haughtiness. The Nurse could feel her wrath and moved to her side, touching her gently to soothe her as she moved her off to one side. The ifrit was standing before the Dyer's Wife, his eyes fixed on her, while she kept hers lowered.

"Here you are before me," he said in a voice that sounded beguiling, almost submissive, deeper and more striking than the Empress would have expected, "you exquisite one, you who are waiting for me."

"Waiting?" said the woman. "I, waiting for you?"

"You are a woman, but he who is meant to unravel the knots of your heart was never near you before this hour."

The woman opened her mouth, but no sound came out. His hands were resting on her knees as he slithered closer to her; there was something of the panther and something of the serpent about him. The Empress felt her soul being torn.

"Help her ward off this fiend," she whispered to the Nurse. "Don't you see she doesn't want him?"

"Score a bull's-eye but not damage the disc—that would be a splendid feat!" the Nurse answered coldly.

With both hands, the ifrit took hold of the woman's wrists and forced her to look up at him, but her glance could not withstand his as it pierced deep, revealing everything about her to the depth of her heart.

"His eyes—tell him to turn away his eyes," the Dyer's Wife called out, and it looked as if she was trying to flee.

But the ifrit stayed close by her, his hands at rest on the

back of her neck, and the words that were pouring so swiftly from his lips sounded flattering and threatening at the same time. The Empress was trying not to look, but she was forced to. She did not understand what she was seeing, but yet it wasn't altogether perplexing, for an oppressive sense that it was all real held the moment fast.

"Let it be over!" she sighed and hid her face in a sack of dried herbs. "What is he to her, what is she to him that they should meet and come together? Why is she fighting against him in such a half-hearted way? What is at issue between these two creatures?"

"Your shadow is at issue," was the Nurse's answer, and her face lit up.

"No, not that," the Empress exclaimed into the old woman's ear.

"Quiet!" said the old one, "quiet. She is full of disdain and must be consumed in the fire of longing."

"Tempt her with treasures; she spoke of sumptuous banquets. She wants a house and slaves," said the Empress. "Give her anything she wants, but not that!"

"Try to hook with a bent nail, and you will be sure to fail," the old one answered with her glib tongue. "It must have a barb."

The Dyer's Wife had wrenched her hands free and stood up. "I want to hide," she said, "help me, old one. I want to hide from him! What has this stranger to do with me? No matter if he's handsome!"

The Nurse was quickly at her side. "Not to remain a stranger to you, oh radiant one," she said with an indescribable expression, "is all that he craves."

"I want to hide from his gaze," the woman cried out,

shoving the old woman aside so clumsily that she was now closer to the man than before. "Ask him how he even dares to ask of me what he has asked of me, a man I did not even know an hour ago! Ask him! He says he is asking it as a pledge of my trust, an outward sign that my heart is not shallow!"

"Verily he is speaking the truth," cried the Nurse with eagerness, exchanging a look with the ifrit. "And not having known him an hour ago is just one more reason to bestow yourself bountifully on him. That is how it is meant to be from heart to heart, and anyone who taught you differently had no other aim than to deceive you outright, artless one."

"So it is," cried the ifrit, but the Nurse signaled him to be silent. She was straining herself to listen to something outside.

"You must part, loving ones," she cried, "I hear the foot-steps of the Dyer making his way home. He is glad of heart and is carrying an earthenware bowl in his hands."

The Empress's heart began beating for joy; she could hardly wait to see that strong and sturdy man walk in.

"Why doesn't he fling the door wide open? Why doesn't he come walking right in?" she thought as she raised her head.

Something that sounded like music was coming from out-side, something like discordant singing. The Nurse was now standing next to her and casting a strange look her way.

"Rouse yourself and tell them to separate for today," she said, "it is time now."

The ifrit had put his arm around the waist of the Dyer's Wife and was trying to pull her away with him; it looked as if he were tugging at her with all the danger that the force of redoubled brazenness could lend him. He was on the verge of hauling away his prey through the air, high over the heads of those entering the house; he was all the more handsome as he gnashed his teeth with impatience. The Empress stepped directly into his path. Her courage was equal to his; she put both her arms around the Dyer's Wife, whereupon the ifrit turned his face toward her. It blazed up like an open fire, and out of his eyes, one notably larger than the other, there flashed the hideously grinning abyss of a place never to be set foot in; she was seized with horror, not for herself but for the soul of the Dyer's Wife, who seemed fated to lie in the arms of such a fiend and mingle her breath with his. She wanted to draw the other woman to her, not even aware that she was reaching out to hold a human being in her arms for the first time. The Dyer's Wife hung limply on her arm, bereft of willpower; all she could do was keep her eyes trained on the ifrit, transfixed by him. A mighty wave of feeling passed through the Empress from head to foot. She hardly knew any longer who she was and had no idea how she had come to be in this place. She realized she was being assailed by weakness; even her pure, engaging strength was beginning to fail as her thoughts, in disarray for the first time, were drifting hither and thither in search of help. Inside she was crying out fervently for Barak the Dyer, and she could feel that he was approaching step by step. Now he came into the room, exuberant and full of noise, loaded with provisions and surrounded by company. His face was bright red from happiness and excitement, and he was holding in both hands an enormous bowl heaped with delicious food of all kinds: tender pullets on a bed of rice, preserved meats wrapped in young vine leaves, pumpkin spiced with pistachios, and tenfold more enticing delicacies. The hunchback, crowned with flowers and playing a mouth harp, pushed past him, the one-armed brother was dragging an immense earthen carboy filled with wine, and the one-eyed was bearing on his shoulders the very lamb, now skinned, whose gentle eyes had drawn the Empress's glance the day before, when they were arriving. Crowds of children, followed by famished dogs, had gathered by the door, attracted by the mouth harp and the aroma of such succulent food. Everybody came pouring into the room while the ifrit vanished in a split second, the cloth hanging on poles began swaying, and a tethered goat got loose. The Nurse clapped her hands in greeting and bowed to the master of the house with hypocritical deference. His wife, only half conscious, pulled herself together, and with a wild look around the room that recognized no one—not her brothers-in-law, not even her own husband—wrenched back with fierce breathing and pounding of her trembling heart the soul that had almost departed from her body. But so joyous was the unsuspecting heart of the Dyer over the remarkable luxuries he'd brought home and the festive preparations for a meal such as had never been enjoyed in his modest house that he remained unaware of the upheaval his wife was enduring.

"How about all this, my precious wife," he called out to her in a powerful voice, "what do you say about a banquet like this, after being finicky and refusing the noon meal? What do you think now, with everything spread out before you?"

Because she kept standing there with her eyes wide open and not saying a word, staring at him as if he were a ghost, he thought that amazement and happiness had struck her speechless and could not help laughing.

"Tell her about all we bought, my brothers, so she can see how well we provide. How did it go at the butcher's? And how did it go in the spice shop?"

"Butcher, carve a cut of veal!," sang the hunchback. "And

a haunch of mutton, then show us your chickens!" the one-eyed and the one-armed brother joined in. "And roast-meat man, start turning the spit!" they all bellowed together, as the one-armed brother produced a hefty turning spit that he had attached to the side of his loincloth.

"Roast-meat man, bring out your spit!" the children cried with delight and crowded in from the door.

"And how was it with the rest of the food and the wine?" Barak shouted louder and happier than all the rest.

"It was like this: 'Baker, bring out all your best,'" answered his brothers, 'and choice wine only, you shady merchant!'"

"Yes, that how it was," the Dyer called out proudly, turning his joyfully ruddy face to one and all in turn.

He went up to his wife, drew her close, and covered her mouth and cheeks with kisses. The Nurse leapt in quite close and doubled over with laughter. She had her hand in everywhere, pushing and shooing back the children, now constantly underfoot as they rummaged in the large bowl and reached for burning splinters of firewood in their effort to touch the dead lamb. The hunchback was playing the mouth harp with one hand and helping to fix the lamb onto the spit with the other. The one-eyed brother was pouring wine into small crocks and trying, without much success, to catch some of it in his outstretched mouth. Barak was sitting on the ground in front of the earthenware bowl filled with food; he had drawn his wife down onto his knee and was caressing her, feeding her the choicest morsels he had plucked out of bowl for her and then taking turns raining kisses on her and squeezing her over and over in his powerful embrace. He did not notice how she was choking on the food and remaining as rigid as a corpse through his caresses. From time to time, since she was eating the delectable food so slowly, he would stuff the mouths of the children surrounding him while himself eating just a little here and there, with not much attention.

"Baker, bring out all your best!" the children cried as they cast challenging looks at the one-armed and the one-eyed brothers.

"If ever we buy, we buy the best!" sang the hunchback, reaching with his long arms past everybody into the middle of the bowl.

"O day of joy, O evening of mercy!" Barak sang in his booming voice and reached out with his left hand, which was free, for the smallest of the children and then for another one, taking hold of them firmly by the back of their garments, guiding them cautiously onto his wife's knee while laughing out loud for happiness. The woman abruptly pulled herself up and shoved the children away from her so that they rolled quite close to the open fire; she pushed Barak away so hard that he stumbled onto the large bowl and smashed it with his leg. The bigger children cried out and pulled the smaller ones away from the fire. The one-eyed brother cast around among them and rescued whatever food there was to rescue. The Nurse stopped turning the lamb on the spit and leapt over to the Dyer's Wife, who was hunched on her knees and flailing at the empty air with her hands; a long, piercing scream was forced out of her mouth. The two kinswomen quickly carried the Wife to her bed; by now she was twitching and shuddering. Barak was by their side but didn't trust himself to touch his screaming wife; he ran back to the fire and looked in total bafflement at the food, then dashed back over to the bed and fearfully touched his wife, who was thrashing wildly about like a fish on dry land. He thought she might be poisoned. He handed a cloth to the old woman and shoved his brothers and the children out the door. They snatched the lamb from the spit, and the sharp smell of burning fat filled the room.

The Dyer's Wife had stopped screaming, but now a spasm convulsed all her limbs. She gnashed her teeth at her husband when she caught sight of him and panted as she said to the Nurse, "Get me away from here; the ways are known to you. Swear to me I will never again have to see this house and that face."

The Nurse stretched out three fingers and then drew back one of them, drawing attention to the remaining two with a furtive glance. The Dyer's Wife closed her eyes; Barak had not heard what they were saying but saw the Nurse whispering to her and the woman answering weakly, though her mouth was no longer clenched; she gradually grew calmer and lay there peacefully.

Chapter Four

On the evening of the third day the hunting party was making its way upwards along the slope of a deep valley which narrowed more and more to a ravine. The ravine grew steep and almost fathomless in depth. Down below surged foaming water; up above, past a tall stone bridge spanning the abyss, lay a solitary village, now fully taken over by the huntsmen. The Emperor came riding over the stone bridge, holding his horse to the pathway as the men behind him leapt from their saddles, expecting him to dismount. Two of the highest-ranking retainers hurried over and held the Emperor's bridle and stirrups, but he waved them away with a casual gesture of his fine, slender hand and remained in the saddle. The jester had only been waiting for this moment to start his antics, hoping in a cajoling way to offset the Emperor's present state of distress by crudely baiting the village bumpkins. He suddenly leapt up close to the Emperor's horse from the side, pulling behind him by his long, yellowish-white beard an old man who was acting cowed.

"Now, elder statesman of this accursed village," he shouted at the man, "kneel down right here and confess that you mountain villagers are all infamous thieves who know how to lure falcons by using a hooded bird as bait; admit that you're all fanatical about hunting with falcons; you're all poachers and bird thieves from the minute you're born; confess that every one of you would sell your own mother or even your wedded wife if it could make one of the Emperor's red falcons fall into your hands—God forbid!—because your greedy kind consider the women a fair trade for a goshawk trained to kill sparrows!"

The old man's eyelids were twitching; he took this all at face value and was having visions of imminent death; he raised his hands beseechingly and was picturing them chopped off or mutilated. He wanted to deliver a speech, but the iron voice of the jester and the forbidding appearance he knew how to assume dashed the old man to the ground. With a glance begging for help he looked up at the figure above him on the horse, but the mounted man did not move or give him even a fleeting glimpse in return.

"By my eyes," cried the old man in desperation, "and may I be blinded on the spot! We are lowly shepherds who know nothing about hunting and cannot tell the difference between a falcon and a crow!"

He thrust his hands out into the air in fear, but so close to the horse's eyes that the animal reared up high; with his right hand the Emperor quickly snatched at the case protecting the Empress's letter, which he was carrying under his garments. Only then did he grasp the bridle and calm the horse. The jester, who was eagerly hanging on the Emperor's features for any sign of a smile or nod, did not receive even a glance; instead, the Emperor's eyes were staring straight ahead like those of a drowsy eagle. It was full afternoon, and the air here in the innermost domain of the Seven Mountains of the Moon was so clear that the Emperor could distinguish at a great distance the source of the river surging far below his feet. He saw where it began as a waterfall, slender as a thread, high up on the rock face and from that height plummeted down into a small forest. On the highest treetop in those woods he could see a falcon sitting with a bird in its claws and plucking it.

The Emperor signaled to the head falconer and pointed out the sight to him by a mere nod; with his observant eyes that stood far apart, the falconer had caught sight of the bird long before and realized that the one perched far up there on a limb was not the one they were looking for, the one it was his highest obligation to find and entice back, so that while his face—ruddy above and below the large scar across his nose—grew even darker, he turned it away in shame. Meanwhile, the Emperor's features clouded over as he leaned down slightly toward the falconer.

"On this hunting ground we must find and recapture the red falcon—both you and I, or on your head be it," he said softly.

The falconer did not dare look his lord in the face but kept his eyes fixed on the Emperor's chest; he turned pale yellow, and his widely spaced eyes took on a frightened expression. He stepped away and had two mules brought up, chose a loden coat and a leather coat, and attached two leather pouches to his pack, one of them with air holes like a cage. The Emperor had leapt down from his horse and swung himself up onto one of the mules without touching the stirrup. The head falconer mounted the other one but had to hold on to the pommel, because his limbs felt as if they were paralyzed. Even more than his lord's wrath or the ominous threat, he feared being alone with him. Helplessly he turned in his saddle and saw the riding master beckon one of his underlings; the falconer tossed the coats to the boy as if he had been waiting to do so. The lad had been watching eagerly and had made his way to the fore with deliberate intent; his eyes were shining as he nimbly jumped up onto the third mule and went trotting along behind the other two.

They rode silently along the ravine, and the path led quickly to the heights. They went in single file, the mules placing their hooves between boulders and tree roots. The riders had one knee over the abyss while the other scraped against the ivy clutching the black rock face. Small birds eyed them from their nests higher up and darted quickly past their chests. The falconer kept his eyes fixed on the Emperor's back; his lord's shoulders and neck looked solid as a rock, unapproachable, pitiless. Somewhat higher up, the Emperor got down from his mule, and the lad, quick as a cat, jumped off his as well. The Emperor didn't even notice him, but the boy was blissful at being alone with his august lord, for the falconer had crept off to the side, his eyes constantly looking up at the sky. The Emperor looked down: a surpassing radiance lay over the mountains and valleys; here and there, waterfalls plunged, brilliantly gleaming into the valley below, as from the deepest canyons a blue-tinged mist began rising. Mountain crests crossed in the distance, and dark forests stood on the slopes, but up above, everything was barren and rugged. Not one of these cliffs was like any other, and yet they all merged and blended together in luminous brilliance like the marks in the Empress's letter, all of them wondrously beautiful, none of them resembling another, with neither beginning nor ending to be seen, since the end intertwined itself with the start, quite as if untold depths of diffidence and modesty precluded anything so bold as direct address. Now a strong, pure scent, like that wafting up from the ravines, made its way from the letter to him who was meant to read it. Remembrance caused the Emperor to close his eyes involuntarily, and the young lad could now read the gentleness and compassion in his face. Happiness swept through the Emperor; for sheer delight he broke off a tree branch and hurled it away. They rode into the woods and made their way among the trees along the water, heading for a pond.

The falconer stayed behind and for the hundredth time scanned the sky, still bright and now flooded with the moon's first light. He saw the sun setting opposite, between two mighty rocks, thrusting upwards from the highest Moon Mountain; its last ray reached across the sky and the abyss, black by now, and then single clouds here and there began creeping like snakes out of the crevices. He let out a sigh: he had scant expectation and was setting his hopes on the following day, though not willing to let any chance pass by now. He opened one of the leather pouches he had tied to his saddle belt and drew out from it a small rust-colored bird, which was fiercely resisting and ruffling its feathers. Wrinkling his brow, the falconer tied the bird to a thorn bush with a leather strap.

"Get on with it," he said. "Your eyes are keener than the keenest eyes of others. Give me tidings of the one I am eager to find, and give me tidings quickly, or it will be your death. For just as he who has gone is over me, so I am over you."

A short time went by, and then the bird began tugging at its restraint in anguish as it uttered piercing cries of fear. The falconer could hardly contain himself for unrest and expectancy. He flung himself to the ground behind the thorn bush and imitated three times and more the call of the wood dove. The male doves came flying from out of the forest, near the water, in search of the female calling out. And within a short time, there appeared high up in the sky a bird that kept growing larger and larger.

"There you are," cried the falconer enraptured, "you remember your keeper; you have come back to the hand that first reached out to feed you."

He undid a small drum from his belt and tapped out a special summons with his knuckles.

"You recognize your call," he cried. "Yes, you've come back to your own again, and we ask your forgiveness! We have offended against your peerless dignity and now, although we do not know why, you have magnanimously forgiven us!"

The bird tied to the thorn bush was trying in its fear to sink deeper into its branches, the doves went flying off in every direction, and the falcon hurtled down in a straight line, hovering in the air, wings outspread, just above the falconer; then without moving its wings, it darted on a slant toward the woods. The falconer's heart was standing still; it seemed to him that the falcon, its eyes wide open and glinting red, had looked at him wrathfully and majestically. But it was the same falcon, every feature of the magnificent bird unmistakable.

The falconer bounded so hastily into the woods after the bird that the tethered mules pulled back with a start. Everything was at stake for him now; he was both amazed and afraid that he could not find the Emperor. The waterfall cascaded silently down from the rock face, and in the pond was reflected an expanse of sky with the falcon, now circling tranquilly over the tree tops. From time to time it would let out a sharp cry, as if impatient at not seeing its master and not wanting to be captured by an inferior. Quiet as an owl, the serving lad was squatting across from the waterfall; there was nothing to be gotten from him except that the Emperor had gone inside up there. He pointed to a cave high up on the rock face, the entrance hardly more than a man's height, its crumbling threshold wet with spray from the waving falls. A few steps led upward from the water; they seemed hewn and polished by human hands, though they were ancient. The boy saw the Emperor talking to himself and then reaching out to lay aside his outer garment; the lad was fearful but heavy-eyed with fatigue as well, and it felt to him, as he saw the moon shining down on him like a lantern, as if he had been forgotten on the threshold of the imperial bedchamber. He deliberately closed his eyes and fell asleep to the constant sound of water. Then the Emperor had suddenly been standing before the lad, shaking him awake and asking him if he heard singing. He had heard it very close by and then farther off. The Emperor had then suddenly turned his back and hurriedly made for the cave. At first the boy didn't dare venture after the Emperor without being bidden, but then he'd crept along behind until the Emperor was no longer to be seen. The cavern had to be an old vaulted roof; its walls had been hewn out of the rock, and it seemed there was another exit. He had waited a long time for the Emperor to return. The falconer hardly listened to the lad; he could not begin to estimate the time that had passed while he was trembling with anticipation that the falcon might come back, but the bird was again taunting him by constantly calling to him. Now the beautiful falcon flew high up and looked down at him after perching on the topmost bare branch of an oak tree struck by lightning but still sending out leaves lower down. The falconer stood as if rooted to the spot, finally tearing himself loose and crouching along; he could see his hand in front of him, red, as if it had been cut off, when he began climbing the tree and reaching out in vain to catch hold of the falcon at the very moment when the Emperor emerged from inside the mountain and the wicked bird mockingly soared upward, out of reach for good. The lad was running silently beside the falconer. The falcon spread its wings, flew toward them as if in greeting, but then with a single beat of its wings tore itself away, upward and to the side, then whooshed back downward and, with a cry mingling happiness and scorn, bolted directly into the mountain face through the waterfall foaming with spray. Endowed with some mysterious power, it must have known there was an entrance there, hidden though it was by the plummeting water. The falconer gnashed his teeth in impotent rage and rolled his eyes helplessly. He was confronted with an impish grin that covered the boy's features, perhaps brought on by awkwardness at the falcon's unexpected move. Infuriated, the falconer slapped him full in the face. The boy leapt into the underbrush and crouched there, but in the depth of his soul he was happy at having received the undeserved blow; a smile came over his face, happy and beaming, as he silently waited among the bushes for his lord to come back.

The Emperor quickly descended the steep, even steps, not heeding the door at his back; the voices he now heard singing, the extraordinary atmosphere, and the circumstances by which he had come to this place were holding all his senses spellbound. Everything penetrated deeply into him here; this was the place of his first adventure with the woman he loved. That unforgettable first hour of love was present to him now, stirring up his blood so that he did not feel the strange chill, as of the grave, seeping out of the mountain wall and the floor of the cavern to pierce him through. There would have been no room inside him for a new adventure—or perhaps there might. Who could say? No particular thought or image came to him, but everything he was sensing was intimately connected with his beloved. He could not understand the words of the song. As he went down each step, he kept thinking the meaning would come clear to him on the next one down. He kept hearing a certain frequently repeated line. He hurried down the last steps more quickly and found himself in a kind of dimly lit entrance hall; the light was coming from underneath a door on the opposite side, one made of massive wood with ornate decorative strips. He could not find a lock or a handle, but as he walked closer to the door, its panels moved on their hinges. At that moment he could clearly hear the last of those words that had recurred so often. They were: "What boots it? We shall not be born!"

He was in too great a hurry to think about what these words meant. He stepped across the threshold, and the double doors at once quietly clicked shut behind him. He was standing in a spacious chamber whose walls seemed to him to be made of nothing other than the smooth stone of the mountain. In the middle of the chamber was a table set for two guests, one at either end. At each side of the table six tall lamps were glowing with soft but festive light. There was no decoration or implement of any kind on the walls, and yet the whole place conveyed a strange opulence that caused the Emperor's chest to narrow. A boy was moving back and forth between the table and the part of the chamber lying opposite the door. He must have been the one who was singing. He brought serving dishes that seemed to be made of solid gold as well as long-necked pitchers set with precious stones and arranged them on the table. Several of the serving vessels, especially those with covers, were so heavy that he carried them on his head, not in his hands, but as gracefully as a young deer. The boy stepped out of the darkness and into the light and did not seem surprised when he saw the Emperor standing by the doorway. He clasped his hands at his chest and bowed.

To the rear a voice called out, "Now it is time!"

But this part of the chamber was in semi-darkness, and only later could the Emperor make out that there was a door on that side, too, exactly like the one behind him, the one he had entered by, and standing directly opposite. The loud cry echoed and died away on every side, revealing how large the chamber was. The youth bowed all the way to the ground before the Emperor without saying a word. Then with a gesture of the deepest respect he pointed toward the seat at the upper end of the table. Even though all twelve lamps ranged along both sides of the table were burning uniformly, the light streaming from the upper end must somehow have had a stronger quality, illuminating the place there and its resplendent setting with brilliant radiance; the middle of the table was more gently and simply lit, while the lower end lay in russet twilight. The youth cast an observant look at the Emperor, but his mouth stayed completely closed. A moment passed before it dawned on the Emperor that it was up to him to speak the first words.

"What have we here?" he asked. "Have you prepared such a banquet for one who simply happened along?"

The handsome youth's tightly closed lips parted; he seemed timid and stepped off to the side, looking around as he did. But the Emperor was no longer paying attention to him, for three figures, whom he could not stop looking at, had in some way stepped out of the wall sideways. The middle one was a beautiful young girl who did not so much step toward the Emperor as glide up to him; two young boys were walking beside her but could hardly keep up; their beauty resembled that of the youth who had set the table, but these boys were smaller and more childlike. The girl was carrying a rolled-up carpet, which she spread out before the Emperor, bowing almost completely to the ground as she did so.

"Forgive, O great Emperor," she began—and only now, as she stood at her full height, did he see that despite her child-like delicacy she was not much shorter than he—"forgive," she said, "my not having heard your approach, engrossed as I was in weaving this carpet. But if you should find it worthy to lie at your feet during a repast for the inadequacy of which we ask your indulgence, then the thread at the end will not be cut off but looped back to join the thread at the beginning instead."

She brought forth her words with lowered eyes; the reso-nant timbre of her voice bore so deeply into the Emperor's soul that he almost missed their meaning. The carpet lay before his feet; he saw only a part of it, and the rear side at that, but still he had never set eyes on anything like this woven fabric, in which moon crescents, star clusters, tendrils and flowers, humans and animals all merged and blended. He could hardly force his glance away, and it took an effort for him to call to mind the dictates of courtesy. A short time passed, then, before he addressed some words to the unknown young girl.

"You are on a journey, I presume," he said with great but benign condescension, careful to avoid sounding in any way overbearing. "Have you pitched your tents and those of your entourage somewhere nearby? And have you sought out this ancient vaulted cavern because it is cooler here? So I gather, at any rate. It would displease me to hear that you dwell inside this mountain!"

The children hung on his words with the greatest attention. As he spoke this last sentence, which passed his lips with an involuntary note of greater severity, a light spasm of laughter crossed their faces. It was obvious that the three boys were struggling to keep from laughing out loud. The girl regained her composure at once, however, and her features again took on an expression of utmost attention, not to say gravity.

"Or is your father's dwelling nearby?" asked the Emperor; nothing about him revealed that he had noticed their unseemly behavior.

The three boys had to fight even harder not to laugh, and now the one who had set the table bent over hastily, finding something to set to rights, as a way of hiding his face.

"Who is your father, you beautiful ones?" asked the Emperor for the third time, his composure intact; only those who knew him well could have detected by the slight shaking of his voice how exasperated he was becoming.

The beautiful girl was the first to venture an answer.

"Forgive us, august lord," she said, "and do not be offended by my young brothers, lacking as they do all experience in the art of polite conversation. We must nonetheless request that you deign to accept for a short time still such meager fare as we are able to offer, for it seems our oldest brother does not yet have in complete readiness all the courses and dishes he considers worthy of being set before you."

Her gestures were inviting him to approach the table, and he now felt nearly weak with hunger, but the poised bearing of the young people and the incredible gracefulness of all their movements made it impossible for him to turn his thoughts elsewhere. The girl had knelt down at the upper end of the table, spreading out the carpet and inviting him to sit down. On it, now beneath his feet, flowers blended into animals, huntsmen and lovers emerged from the exquisitely rendered creeping vines, falcons hovered above the scene like soaring blossoms, and everything was interlinked with everything else. The whole was a glorious marvel, though a chill mounted from it to his hips.

"How did you manage to create this carpet in such perfection?" He turned to the girl, who in her modesty had taken several steps back.

She immediately lowered her eyes but answered with no hesitation. "When I weave, I cut from the cloth whatever is beautiful; that which merely entices the senses and lures them to ruin I leave out."

The Emperor looked at her. "How do you go about it?" he asked, feeling what an effort it was to remain collected, all the more since every object his eye encountered was borne in on him with wonderful sharpness; he now could see more and more of what was in the chamber and thought objects were growing more distinct with his every breath.

"How do you go about it?" he asked again. The young lady followed his glance with delight. Some time passed before she answered.

"I proceed when weaving," she said, "as does your exalted eye when looking. I do not see what is, and I do not see what is not; I see instead what always is, and I weave in view of that."

But he did not hear her, so lost was he in the sight of the magnificent walls from which the lamplight was reflected. He realized from the expectant look with which the boys turned to him that he needed to answer. He was deeply absorbed by the beauty of their faces, aglow in a way he thought he had never seen in children's faces before, and in their eyes, focused on him so intently, he saw something he had never at any time discerned in anyone else's eyes.

"Are there more of you brothers and sisters?" he abruptly asked the boy standing closest to him. He did not know why just this question and no other had come from his mouth. His eye hung entranced on their figures. The desire to possess them suffused him from head to toe, and he had to keep himself under strict control so as not to touch them.

"That depends on you"—the answer came not from the boy he had asked, but from one of the other ones.

Now the Emperor turned to him and could feel in himself how strongly he was endeavoring to give a jovial tone to his question.

"Is your house nearby or far away? Are you going onward? Was it something good or something bad that made you run away?"

The boy did not offer an answer but instead looked over to the one who had set the table. Once more, it took some effort for them to suppress their laughter. The Emperor sat up somewhat straighter in the cushions, richly embroidered with pearls, against which he was leaning. Just changing his position cost him an exceptional effort; a feeling of coldness that started in his hands and feet was making its way to his heart. He looked sharply at the children.

"Did you know beforehand that we were going to meet?" he asked again, without addressing anyone in the group individually. "Is this the end of a journey or a beginning? Is there more lying before you or behind you"?

The tone of his voice sounded harsher in this tall chamber than he had wanted it to, and his questions followed in quick succession.

"You lie before us, and you lie behind us!" called the oldest youth, the table setter, very loudly, making a deep bow before the Emperor as he did so; his hands, in which he was holding a golden ladle, reached down toward the ground.

One of the smaller boys darted over to the Emperor, stood very close to him, looked him deep in the eye, and with feigned seriousness said, slowly and with emphasis, "Your questions reveal no more insight, O great Emperor, than do those of a small child. Tell us this, if you will: when you go to the table, do you do so to remain within satiation or to release yourself from it? And when you go on a journey, is it so that you can remain away or return home?"

"What manner of talk is that?" cried the girl as her eyes widened. "Hither and stand behind me!"

The young boy leapt to her side and kept on kissing her flared sleeves with respect and contrition; the other one did likewise, even though she had not grown angry with him. She did not turn toward either of them but imploringly raised her hands in fear toward the Emperor.

"O how can we gain your grace and favor, we who are so imperfect!" she cried, full of fear. The Emperor saw only her hand, incomparably beautiful and translucently lustrous like alabaster.

"You are the ones I must possess and hold," he cried out, "regardless of the means!"

Her hand flinched as her eye met his with indescribable hesitancy and awe; he regretted his arrogant words and even more the unconcealed fierceness of his tone and now quickly added in a more gently pressing voice, "By what means can I be united with you forever? For that is what I desire, even were I called on to give my heart's blood!"

The girl visibly took fright once more. It seemed as if this question was too powerful for mere words, as if she were capable of answering only with her eyes.

"I am accustomed to obtaining whatever I desire!" cried the Emperor.

Her entire soul was looking out from her eyes, and she fixed the Emperor with a steady glance in which were mingled awe, tenderness, and nameless dread. It was so intense that the Emperor lowered his eyes so he could collect himself to ask a crucial question; he felt it hovering at the edge of his lips, but he forgot it, for when he raised his eyelids again he saw the entire table covered with flowers gleaming in the lamplight like scattered jewels. He also saw the girl's hand guiding the last of those flowers away from the edge of the table, flowing from her hands and placing themselves in order until they all finally lay arranged like a wonderfully intricate piece of embroidery. He saw her face light up as she lovingly signaled with her eyes to someone who had not been there before and whose height and slenderness of figure resembled hers. Now he noticed at the opposite side of this cavernous chamber a door exactly like the one by which he had entered not long before; its panels were standing open and half-grown children were coming through it two by two with covered bowls in their hands.

"Who is that?" the Emperor asked the girl, turning his eyes toward the person who had not been there before. "Is he the kitchen master, the head steward?"

"Now it is time!" that person cried out, and as if in confirmation, he joined the children carrying the serving vessels as they came closer, still two by two, and served in rotation by having one of the pair move toward the Emperor's place at the upper end of the table and the other toward the opposite end.

"What does that statement mean that I have now heard for a second time?" asked the Emperor. "And why am I being attended to so quickly that I can hardly collect myself? Tell this man to take the time he needs."

"Time?" said the girl, looking at him with an embarrassed expression. "We do not know what that is, but our whole desire is to become familiar with it and to be subject to it."

Her embarrassment made her even more appealing. The Emperor feasted his eyes on her, but there was no trace of cupidity in his enchantment.

The kitchen steward clapped his hands, and the servers leapt aside, forming two lines. A rider now bolted between them like a lightning flash, followed immediately by a second; the first was on a steel-gray horse, the other on a fire-colored steed. Each was carrying before him on the pommel of his saddle a covered bowl made of gold and ornamented with precious stones. Each reined in his horse, and one of the serving children hastened to them, relieving them of their bowls with utmost gravity and presenting them to the Emperor while kneeling on the spot. The riders drew out their scimitars and hailed the Emperor by riding straight toward him but then leaping out of their saddles, quick as lightning, and striking the floor to the left and right of the table with the tips of their sabers to produce a ringing sound. The Emperor's very soul blazed forth in his eyes; what delighted him above all was the fraternal similarity between these youthful riders and the more childlike boys who had been bearing him company all along. More than anything, he wanted now to speak to these horsemen; he looked at them most affably and cordially, beckoning them to come closer. But it was all in vain. As if they did not understand that he was eager for their company, they set their horses to stepping backwards along the smooth stone floor, handling the reins with captivating style as they retreated ever farther until the mounts' rear hooves were almost grazing the wall. Then they tugged the reins gently, making the horses rear up high; their forehooves pawed the air, but they looked more like birds in the dexterity with which they craned their necks and tossed their own weight about like bright-scaled fish in the moonlight, one on the left side of the chamber, the other on the right. The faces of these young riders were tense, but over their features lingered a silver smile they directed toward the Emperor all the while. It was clear that their task was completed and that they were about to vanish from the cavern chamber but that out of deference they did not want to turn their backs on their guest. They glided straight through the wall, though there was no way to see how the wall parted. Their smile was the last thing that shone out like a beam of reflected light.

"Where have they gone?" the Emperor shouted as a sharp pain passed through him. He could not grasp how a sight that had so quickly captivated him could so quickly have dissolved into thin air.

All this time, the girl's eyes remained fixed on him with the same delight; she seemed now to be imbibing the expression of wonderment in his face, and she cried, "Is this, O great Emperor, not comparable to my carpet, with its curving, interlinking patterns, which found favor in your august eye? Did you find contentment in the display proffered you by my second and third brothers?"

"They are in all truth very comparable," replied the Emperor breathlessly. "But why that haste?" he cried, a loud sigh forced from him against his will. "How are unfledged children suitable companions for me? Those two riders should be sitting beside me, one to my left and the other to my right, and I wish to see them again, for each has taken a piece of my body with him!"

No one answered. The younger children walked back and forth serving him, and the table setter presented the dishes. Others came in as well and handed their bowls to the ones carving and serving; never in all the coming and going did one bump into another, for the steward was guiding everyone with his keen but somber looks. Still others were present, too, invisible like shadows, who passed the serving vessels out of the darkness; it would not have been possible to say who and how many were in the room and how many not. Left and right they knelt down in turn with the dishes, and now a young girl appeared. This child was carrying a heavy golden bowl she could barely keep a grip on; tense with exertion, she was forcing herself not to tremble.

"How are you able to do this, you small, delicate child?" asked the Emperor.

"To serve is the one way to rule; there is no other, great Emperor," the child answered; over the bowl and below her finely drawn eyebrow he was met by a look far beyond her years.

He felt an impulse to answer her, but his attention was just then seized by a boy kneeling at his other side, one of those who had been with the older girl earlier and now holding out to him a deep bowl set with precious stones that was full to the brim with preserved spices. He could not resist openly showing these beautiful children the feeling that now pulsed through all his veins; he wanted to keep them close by him, even if it meant throwing the orderly arrangement of the table and everything else into confusion. He reached left and right for both bowls, each holding aromatic sweets concocted of fruits and spices.

"Set your bowls on the ground," he commanded, "and raise your faces to me."

He tried to fill the children's mouths with this exquisite fare, but they leaned backwards and refused the food with imploring gestures. He reached out to them but was reaching into empty space; his outstretched hand and face felt only a draft of icy air, as when a door to the outside has opened. The children were now quite far off, and they looked over toward him with a stern glance. Their faces, as he looked at them sideways, appeared much older to him, the girl's eyebrows sharper and in some way alien, as though her every breath required a year. They mingled among the throng of servers, and as they joined the others, they again looked childlike. The Emperor was more dismayed than he had ever been.

"Who am I?" he asked himself, and "How did I get to this place?" His throat was parched, and he instinctively reached for the heavy gold goblet standing before him. His lips were soothed by a cool, lightly fragrant drink of something he had never tasted before.

He drank thirstily but quickly regained control, and he called out as he lifted the drinking vessel, "I drink to you! You understand how to give a feast! All honor and praise for this encounter and the astonishing cultivation you have all acquired!"

"Everything is astonishing in your presence," answered the girl, who was standing motionless behind him, "and this moment in time, during which you are our guest, is above all other moments for us," as her face took on an expression of such great joy that her eyes widened as if in fright.

The Emperor beckoned her closer. Unprecedented feelings of happiness and well-being surged inside him and caused him to forget the cold creeping up to his shoulders and circling his hips like an iron band. He purposely raised and lowered his eyelids a few times before he spoke: "You share knowledge of some mystery, and it could gladden my heart if you were to disclose it to me."

"Between you and us there is but one mystery, that of total reverence," answered the girl.

The Emperor's glance lingered on her without understanding but with all the greater delight, and he kept his head turned toward her; at the same time he saw, without looking away, that someone had knelt down next to him with a new serving vessel, while another lifted the cover. He kept thinking about the answer he had just heard—it seemed to contain more than mere courtesy—while reaching into the serving dish without turning his glance that way.

"You speak of what we are to you, but why do you never ask what you are to us?" the girl said quickly and as softly as a breath.

The Emperor's expression changed; his mouth suddenly fell open and, in the way he bared his teeth for just a second, it betrayed a peevishness that could no longer be held in check.

"I am demanding knowledge from you about how I can bring you to my side forever!" he cried out loudly and commandingly, hardly recognizing his own voice.

Suddenly the girl was right by his shoulder, like a bird, and she bent her face down to him. The beauty of her lightning-quick movement made him blissful.

"At the very moment of our telling you that," she whispered, "you will banish us from your presence forever!"

The steward looked across the table at her; she went over to him meekly and took a position behind her brother near the middle of the table, but off to the side. The Emperor followed her with his glance. He was vexed by the bewildering nature of her answer; his face grew darker at watching her obey someone else's commands in his presence, and he was on the verge of pushing away the table and standing up. Just at that moment the smaller girl walked past him.

She smiled at him as these words crossed her lips in a low voice: "True greatness is humbling of self, O lofty Emperor!" They calmed him at once, so that he looked straight ahead like one dining impassively. So it came about that for the first time since the beginning of the feast he fixed his eyes on the dark end of the table opposite him and with astonishment saw something occurring, the meaning of which he was even less able to grasp than anything before.

He watched the same children who had served him with beaming smiles now kneeling to the left and right of an empty place and with deep solemnity proffering the vessels one by one to a guest who was not there. The standing servers lifted the covers, waited for some time with the same respect they had shown the Emperor, and then covered the dishes again. When the kneeling servers stood up and walked away, their faces were flooded with tears; those standing had tears streaming down their faces as well, and sighs were constantly being forced out of them. Others entered and joined in too, and when they had served the guest who was not there, they also wept and sighed. Their sighs and half-suppressed weeping filled the whole chamber.

He noticed at the same time that the lamps were suddenly shining more dimly, as if they were burning down. He turned to the steward, intending to signal him that he should tend to the lamps, as they were threatening to go out. But he was struck by an expression on the man's face, glancing down and sideways at him, that he had had to withstand only once in his life and thought he would never have to withstand again: it was the look which the bleeding falcon, perched on a tall rock, had trained on his master for the last time, long and piercing, before vanishing into the darkness with spastic, exhausted beats of its wings. It was in great tension that the Emperor bore up under the creature's gaze.

"Who are you?" he cried out. "Hither at my feet!" He did not lower his eyes. The steward slowly turned his away, however, as if disdainfully, and gave a single sign. At once everyone ceased walking back and forth, offering vessels and bowls, lifting covers, and carving. Everywhere they came to a silent standstill. The steward made his way among them without a sound and came up to the Emperor. The princess took a step, as if she meant to move between them, but then she stopped as if bound.

"Who is this man?" the Emperor shouted over his shoulder toward her. "What flagrant audacity in every step he takes! Who made him my judge?" He felt his heart pounding with a dull thud that had caused him to rise slowly to his feet. His limbs were as heavy as if he had to lift a heavy burden from the ground. He turned around and over his shoulder saw the girl standing nearby. Behind her, two figures had stepped out of the wall and were coming toward him, one carrying a golden wash basin, the other a small hand pitcher. When they were standing close to him and preparing to pour water over his hands, he recognized them as the two dashing youths from before, those who had come as intrepid horsemen and had vanished into the wall while mounted on their steeds. The Emperor beckoned to them; eagerly and with a smile he opened out his hands toward them, but they did not seem to know who he was. He opened his mouth to speak, but the words died in his throat. They looked at him sorrowfully, as at a stranger; one held the basin and the other lifted the pitcher. When the water poured out, it struck the Emperor's hands hard and ran down them as if splashing over dead stone. He looked over toward the girl as though seeking to be comforted; she was reaching upward with both hands, her jewel-like face beaming and appearing to point somewhere else where help and comfort were. The Emperor was struggling to shed light inside himself on the meaning of her gesture, but inside him were only dull, blurred feelings, one driving away the other. His complete attention was occupied on realizing that the other man had stood up to full height and was now coming toward him with slow and well-nigh stern footsteps; measured by the dull beating of his heart, it seemed an unbearably long wait until the steward closed the short distance between them. Without looking up, he now felt the man standing right beside him; from very close up there was a coolness wafting toward him from head to toe. Squinting through his eyelids he saw that the creature had snatched at the empty air and was now holding a white linen cloth, drying the Emperor's hands in a deferential attitude. But the fluttering motion of the linen towel made his skin crawl.

"O Emperor," the voice said, so close to his cheek that he could feel the cold breath and began shaking with rage at a degree of disrespect such as he had never been subjected to in his life, "do you not regret that our presenting you with a feast was for naught?" Nothing could compare with the vehemence of the rebuke these simple words contained. His heart squeezed tight while cold tears burst from his eyes and froze on his cheeks. As a sign that he would permit no one to speak to him about his wife and that he would never allow anyone to compel him to surrender anything that belonged only to him, the Emperor kept staring straight ahead. The cold now enveloping did him good for a moment, for nothing could come close to his heart.

At this point the children all around the chamber opened their mouths. "She wishes to come, but she cannot!" they cried out toward him. "Oh if we could but see her face!" they called from every side and again began to sigh and weep.

"What cries of woe are these?" he wanted to call out in a severe voice, but the words would not come from his throat. A wind rose up from the middle of the chamber, a breath of something appalling. He was met at the same time by the voice of the one who stood too close to him the whole time; it was subdued but right next to him. "Scant is the reward to anyone who helps you gain what your heart yearns for! Your red falcon knows that!" The Emperor gnashed his teeth hard at the blatant way in which his first hour of love had been remarked on, an hour which had had no witness on earth other than the noiseless falcon. The silence was once again dreadful. That wind had died down.

"Do you not recognize my oldest brother?" the girl murmured to him. "It is he who struck at her eyes with his wings and so helped you to win her."

The Emperor gave no answer.

"She is searching for the path to us!" the children cried. "Bless her path; it is that which we are asking of you."

"What path do you mean?" the Emperor cried out to them, and at once he was pierced with dull and heavy sorrow at his own words without clearly knowing why.

"What good is it if we say to you what you cannot grasp!" the children responded. "You are carrying her letter over your heart but do not have wit enough to read it."

"What do you mean?" the Emperor cried. As he spoke, he could feel the coldness of his heart.

"If you did you would know of her distress and her woe," they answered. The Emperor involuntarily reached toward his chest but realized nothing could help him now and stopped. "You have not untied the knot of her heart! It is about that which we are weeping. For she must be taken from you and given into the hands of one who is capable of loosening the knot of her heart." The wind had risen once more and was blowing toward him.

"Who has told you all of this?" came from his lips.

"Twelve months have passed, and she casts no shadow!" the children cried.

"Do you know everything, then?" asked the Emperor.

"We know what is needful," the children answered. "You have kept her sequestered behind walls," they called out, their voices changing, "and that is why she had to skulk away like a thief in the night. Like a gazelle panting for thirst she steals away to the houses of men and women!"

"How is it they dare say such things to me?" the Emperor asked. He realized now that their voices were different because they were singing. "This is the song I heard when I was standing outside," he told himself.

"She is performing the duties of a serving maid," the voices went on singing, "but that does not pain her. She is doing so for our sake, and hardly does the sun's light appear than she sits on her bed and cries out with yearning, 'Where are you, Barak? Come to me! For I am guilty of harming you!'"

"You, Barak, I am guilty of harming," they kept repeating with radiant sound that struck against the vaulted ceiling.

"What words are these?" cried the Emperor wide-eyed and with the last breath in his chest, which had grown heavier than stone.

"The all-important ones!" answered the children. The Emperor's chin sank heavily to his chest.

"Alas," he said to himself, "alas, that my jester ever dared speak of my melancholy before I came to know this hour."

"Hail to you, Barak!" sang the children with wonderful sonority, "you are but a poor dyer, but you are great of heart and a friend to those who are to come! We bow down to earth before you!"

The Emperor stood neglected in their midst as they bowed to someone who was not there; the children's beautiful faces came so close to the ground that it lit up like water. The girl was standing to the side. Her gaze remained fixed on the Emperor with an indescribable mixture of love and fear. He turned his eyes toward her once more.

"Answer me," he said. "Who is this Barak and what business does my wife have with him?"

"Oh for just a grain of generous feeling!" the children cried in piercing voices.

"What business?" he asked again, harshly this time, and looked at her only though narrow slits. His eyelids had grown heavier than lead. He waited, but he did not desire an answer.

The girl moved away from the others; it was as if she were gliding toward him, her feet not moving; her troubled face had a look of desiring to reveal to him a wondrous mystery.

"For just a grain of generous feeling!" the voices were crying. He suddenly realized with horror that the girl now resembled his wife in some inexplicable way. Into her eyes there now leapt an expression of utmost fear but of devotion at the same time; she was the reflected image of the gazelle that had been frightened almost to death. He could read in that expression the admission of that which he had hoped never to hear by name and a plea for forgiveness he could not grant. He hated the message and the messenger alike and could feel that his heart had turned fully to stone within him. Without a word his hand sought for the dagger in his belt to throw it at the girl here, since he could not throw it at his wife. Unable to feel it with the fingers of his right hand, he tried to enlist the help of his left, but neither hand obeyed him any longer. For a time now his arms of stone had been clamped rigidly against his hips, also turned to stone, and no sound emerged from his petrified lips.

"Now it is time!" the oldest brother called out in a loud voice. The lamps and the table had vanished in an instant.

"Just one grain of generous feeling, Father!" all those beautiful voices cried fervently once more, but the statue, now standing tall and dark in their midst, could no longer move. All the brothers and sisters moved to and fro like flames as their faces were suffused with a gentle glow. The oldest girl remained within sight longest, her eyes fixed on the statue. The walls drew together, the doors disappeared, and the chamber was now circular. It opened overhead, the stars looked in, those figures had all faded away, and the statue of the Emperor remained alone in the center.

Chapter Five

When the Nurse went in to the Empress before sunrise, she was astonished at finding her charge awake so early and sitting on her low bed. The Nurse knelt down beside her and brought out from behind the bed the alabaster jar containing the black ointment.

"All is well with me," said the Empress. "I have a feeling we will gain the shadow today." Her face was beaming. The Nurse applied twice the amount of the darkening solution.

They descended and went toward the Dyer's house, not approaching from the lane but from the side facing the river, where the Dyer had a half-open shed in which he worked; away from the door stood a ladder leading to the flat roof of the house, where cloth was laid out to dry.

"Wait here," said the Nurse, "let's see what the woman intends to do. It's worth a great deal to see without being seen," as they stepped behind the shed. As if summoned, the Dyer's Wife came out of the house and into the yard. "Do you see how pale and hollow-eyed she looks, even this early?" the Nurse whispered. "That's exactly how we need her today." The Dyer's Wife crossed the yard, paying no attention to anything. She was immersed in gloomy thoughts. When the Nurse and the Empress stepped out from their hiding place, the woman was not at all surprised to see them. She seemed completely unaware that she had not seen them since the night before. She moved aside the reed mat hanging in front of the door and motioned to the Nurse to enter before her.

"Begone," she said, as the Empress was preparing to walk in behind the Nurse. "Away with you," the woman repeated, "make yourself useful to the Dyer and look after the hunchback and the one-eyed one. I detest her with everything in me; don't even mention her to me," she added and gestured for the Nurse to go in alone. She wiped off two wooden benches and took a seat on one of them.

"Here, come sit by me," she said. "At first I thought you were a liar and a windbag, but now I have to apologize. You came along and swore up and down that a man somewhere in this wide world is thinking about me, and then you brought in a total stranger, someone I had never set eyes on." She spoke slowly and emphatically, as if she had already spent a long time pondering her whole situation. "So now I've seen him, and that's all to the good; thank you, my teacher; he's handsome." Saying these words, she buried her face in her hands; it had suddenly taken on a glow. "He wants me, I understand," she added darkly. "So listen now to what I have resolved." She interrupted herself, moved the reed mat aside slightly, and looked across to the Dyer. He had rolled up his trousers as far as they would go, tucked the ends of his shirt into his belt, and was standing in a large vat from which steam was rising. By shifting evenly from one leg to the other he was churning dirt and blood out of a butcher's work clothes. The Empress squatted on her heels and watched him from the side. The one-eyed brother was lying ten paces away and sleeping like a rock while the sun shone directly into his nostrils; the misshapen one had just stood up and was using both hands to try scratching his back with all his might, and the one-armed one lay propped up on his elbows yawning with great pleasure, so that nothing of him could be seen but his maw and the black hair surrounding his head like a bush.

"Look at her crouching there like a toad and not saying a word, just sweating out her poison," the Dyer's Wife said all of a sudden as she tossed the Nurse a harsh look. "What kind of woman is she? Is she untouched, or is there a man she belongs to? Answer me!" But she did not wait for an answer. Her expression changed completely. She smiled, and her voice shook as it took on a childish tone. "You have turned me sick, old woman," she said. "I have heard there are those who for sheer thirst cannot drag themselves to the spring; so it stands with me." She sat down on a sack filled with dried herbs. "But it is not you who have made me sick; it is him," she said as if to herself. "He has turned everything in me upside down, again and again, without ever touching me. Do you have any idea what that means? Who was your lover in days of yore, old woman, and what did he teach you? It is they who are our teachers, after all. Who made you so cunning and self-reliant that a youth like him placed himself at your beck and call?" She kept on talking, as if only to herself, without waiting for an answer. "He taught me both ways of blushing. I shall be in thrall to him all the days of my life." She smiled, but at the same time tears welled up in her eyes, only to dry at once. "He came to me last night," she continued. "Not in person, you fool. But can't a woman lie quiet with her eyes open and dream of something as if it were real? Can't a woman lie on this miserable cot and feel beneath her a bed of antelope leather and over her a mantle of soft sable pelts as light as down? But what good is all that? The splendor doesn't last long, because there then comes a stench like that of a child's corpse lying in a corner behind the bed. That must be done away with." She stood up and moved away. Her face displayed revulsion and horror, as if something like what she described were in fact lying there. Then she once more listened with intense concentration to the sounds outside. A sudden gust of wind moved the reed mat by the door and carried with it a noise that might have been the Dyer's voice but perhaps, too, the voice of a stranger from the other side of the river. She pushed the mat aside and stood in the doorway. The Dyer had spread the cloth from the vat across clean boards and was now applying white clay to it. The Empress was helping him. The blood-colored waste water spilled out of the upturned vat into the gutter. They were busy with the work and did not look up. When the Dyer's Wife called to them, they did not hear her.

The Nurse sidled up to the Dyer's Wife from behind and touched her sleeve deferentially. "Rest yourself now," she murmured, "and think about this coming evening. Your skin will have to be smooth and burnished like gold."

"Barak," the woman called to him, "will you not be leaving the house today to go and sell your wares?" The question she called out was simple, but she loaded it with lacerating scorn and mockery. The Dyer did not answer; he seemed not to have heard.

"This evening you will come to the river with me," muttered the Nurse. "He of whom we know is yearning for the hours of evening and is a hero in the time of twilight."

The Dyer's Wife turned around. "It is not possible that she is your child," she said, casting the Nurse a searching look. "She is unsullied. She does not think many thoughts, but those few gleam on her brow like stars." She fell silent for a moment. "I have given thought to having her hanged!" she cried, laughing in a peculiar way. "And how shall I punish that man because my destiny was to be his? What made him dare to approach me with no fear and touch me with his gross mouth? But that is my concern, not yours. This I will say to you, however, and this is the crux of it—I will do as you are bidding me. So now go and bring the Dyer inside, because I want to have a word with him; he seems to have grown hard of hearing and does not answer when I call."

The Nurse was already standing at the doorway; she wanted to go out and convey the message, but she was seething with curiosity to hear what would come out of the younger woman's mouth next.

"His face was hard," the Dyer's Wife continued with that same peculiar, suppressed laughter, even though her expression remained fixed, "but crafty and forceful like a devil's; arrogance, depravity, and greed were written all over that face, and that is why he suits me. He did not know how to speak, but he knew how to conquer." A smile rose from deep inside her and lit up her darkened face. She was beautiful at this moment, glowing as her young blood pulsed through her, and the Nurse observed her with satisfaction. "No, no," she suddenly cried with passionate delight, "he is beautiful; pay no heed to me, you fool, for he is as beautiful as the morning star, and his beauty is the barb on the hook I swallowed at once. Now I am twisting this way and that while you hold the line in your hands—and you know that!" Softly and gently she leaned on the Nurse's shoulder and let herself be petted like a child. "It is the coming together that is so hard; beginning is the only hard part. My God!"

The Nurse could not understand her. "Why are you concerned?" she cried. "We will find our ways and means!"

The Dyer's Wife shook her head. "What do you think I mean, old woman? I mean something truly different, but how could you ever understand that?" The Nurse looked at her bewildered. "He must come to me without you, without you!" the younger woman cried out to her. "Because I despise you—mark that well—and I hate the malice in me that has dealings with you. You know my baseness and his as well, and you are striving to have dominance over his and mine alike, but nothing will come of it, believe me!"

The Nurse blinked with her lashless eyes as her long, thin tongue angrily darted back and forth in her half-open mouth, but she said nothing and quickly went out into the yard; she found the Dyer after he had just taken out of the curing solution an immense length of cloth made of fine mohair, thirteen ells long and three-and-a-half ells wide, then wrapped the saturated fabric in a protective cloth and began to hoist the dripping burden onto his strong back as the Empress, like any serving maid, boosted the enormous bolt of cloth from underneath with all her strength as a way of aiding him in his work.

The Nurse waited but then beckoned, and the Empress hastened over to her. "Is she willing?" she asked at once. "Will she be giving up her shadow?"

"It is not easy for her," was the Nurse's answer. "Those whose coming is not desired are struggling to enter in, and he with the large mouth is their champion, though he is also their destroyer, thank God."

"Yes," said the Empress, but without hearing; she was looking over her shoulder at Barak, who was laboriously hauling his way up the steep ladder, his large and heavy body pressed against the rungs so that his burden might not make him tumble backward. "Make quick work of getting the shadow," she said. "This man should have his reward."

"Reward?" cried the Nurse. "What did that elephant do to earn a reward? But go fetch him and tell him to go into the house. The woman wants to talk to him."

"What are you going to do with them?"

The Nurse contorted her face. "Leave that to me; I can sense them the way a cook can sense when the chicken in the pot is ready." She turned away from the Empress and shuffled back into the house. Silently, the Empress went over to the ladder and climbed the rungs; on the flat roof she found the Dyer still panting and sweating. The sweat mixed with blue dye as it dripped from his face; she wiped it with a small cloth while he delicately separated the hanging strands of blue cloth with his large hands so that air could reach the dye on the inside and in that way turn every part of the dingy yellow-green to a vivid blue. The butcher's clothes were already hanging on the drying pole.

When the Dyer stepped into the house, the Empress was right on his heels and remained standing by the door. The Dyer's Wife bent down as fast as lightning, picked up a dirty chunk of wood off the floor, and hurled it at the Empress with all her might. But that daughter of the spirit world sidestepped it like a puff of air. The Dyer opened his thick lips and started to say something, but his wife shot him a look that made him keep quiet. He bent over and began rummaging among the clutter piled against the wall as if he were looking for something. The Dyer's Wife stayed silent the whole time, but her lovely face now had a dogged and hateful expression. The Dyer rose up on his knees and was turning in his fingers an old ladle made of horn.

"I have carried out many tasks this early," he now said, looking up tenderly at his wife, "and I am thirsty. Give me something to drink." The woman thrust her chin forward; the Nurse hurried to fill an earthen jug with water, which she then held out to the Dyer. He looked at up at his wife as if expecting something, but when she kept gazing past him as if he were not there, he took the jug and drank it dry in one gulp. "What's in that?" he immediately cried with an expression of blissful surprise and toppled backwards in sleep.

The Nurse slunk over to his wife. "I've rid you of your burden," she whispered. "I poured a potion into his drink, even a fourth of which would be enough to fell an elephant for ten hours."

"Accursed one," screamed the Dyer's Wife, "is he to escape me over and over again?" She stepped over to him and looked at him with wrinkled brow.

The Nurse could not understand. "What business do you still have with him?" she asked in bewilderment.

The woman paid no attention to her. She stepped close to the sleeping man's body and looked down at him severely. Then came a sigh from deep within her: "O mother of mine!" and then again "O mother of mine!" She stood there for a long while, looking at him the whole time. "Alas," she said, sighing once more, "if I become the grain, he will be the rooster and will peck and swallow me! If I become fire, he will be water and put me out! For I am shackled to him with iron shackles!" Then she moved away from him but came right back. She nudged his sprawling body with outstretched toes. "To be sure, it is only right"—she was speaking softly but with a very urgent tone—"to put aside those who are not desired, for their outrageous appetites and cravings as they ravage their way through my body makes them murderers, and this man at my feet is their accomplice!" Even as she was whispering these words, she was seized by fearful anxiety; she flung herself down on the prostrate man and tugged at him with all her might. "Barak," she screamed into his ear, "you must heed me, for now is the hour!"

The Nurse sensed that the Empress was standing behind her and wheeled around abruptly; her charge had slipped inside and the Nurse, speechless with astonishment, saw that tears were streaming from her eyes and pouring down her anguished face, as if she were a mortal woman. She took the Empress's hand and lightly shunted her over toward the wall, meeting no resistance. With her foot the Nurse now opened a crude wooden door on its rusty hinges.

"Be quiet and calm now," she murmured, "and know that today, even in this very hour, our concern will end well."

The Empress kept standing there, not making a sound. Bunches of dried plants that hung from the ceiling were brushing against her; the narrow room was crammed with cauldrons and flasks clattering into one another; piled-up sacks of preserved roots kept rustling. The Empress dared not move and was breathing rapidly and fearfully.

"What do you still want from him?" cried the Nurse, tugging the Dyer's Wife away from the sleeping man.

"What do I want?" shrieked the woman. "What does he want, you mean! Who am I, and who is he?" she cried out in contempt, drawing herself to her full height over his body. "How do I come to be with him, and how does he come to be with me? Someone tell me that!" She screamed those words down into the sleeping man's face. He was breathing calmly and not moving. She turned half away in disgust and reached her arm out behind her as if to wrap it around the chest and shoulders of someone who was not there, but her face remained fixed in torment on the Dyer's face. Suddenly she bared her teeth and kicked him hard.

"I do not want this at my back!" she screamed. "Wake him at once."

The Nurse did not know how to get out of the situation; she had to bend to the force of uncontrolled will power. She knelt down and shook the sleeping man gently, breathed on him three times, and blew onto his neck. Barak smiled in his sleep; his lips moved as he said something; his face had the same look as when he chatted with his wife at home or with strangers' children on the street.

"Heed me now," his wife said, bringing her face a little closer to his as his eyes widened into a strange, vacant stare at her. "I am weary of living in your house and seeing nothing but ugliness, and I have found one who will take pity on me. He is offering me untold splendor for all my days. But I must make a sacrifice."

The Empress held her hands over her ears; the words themselves did not penetrate to her, but the tone of voice did, and it sounded odious to her. "Alas," she said to herself, "fish dive deep in the water when they see her, birds take rapid flight, deer dash into thickets, but I had to mingle with them." Her heart beat dully. She tried not to hear anything. But a sound was borne into the deepest part of her, altogether gentle, like a child's voice, and yet it could only have come from the Dyer's mouth. She realized he was talking in his sleep, his tongue slack. Instead of speaking words, he was uttering only a keening, pleasant sound. It was plain to hear that he was talking to children, and his powerful hands were gesturing delicately as he spoke. His wife was looking sternly into the whites of his unseeing, half-opened eyes.

"You're talking," she cried, "so I know you can hear me. Listen, then! They are cast aside—those you are speaking with now are cast aside, I tell you. Do you understand me?"

"Let him be," screamed the Nurse, "what do you think you're doing?"

The Empress could no longer stand seeing that strong man so helpless under the hands of the other two. She opened the door; her eyes widened, and like a firestorm she herself could not contain, her will forced its way over to Barak. The Nurse had no power over her mistress when she stood before her like this; she could only step aside. A jolt ran through Barak's body, and he stood up on his mighty legs but knew nothing of what was around him, as heedless as a dead man. He was being wrenched this way and that and stumbling as if blindfolded. Inside him the poison conjured by magic was battling with the ferociously powerful will of the spirit daughter. What was grossest and lowest in him surfaced, and there came over his face an expression of strength and savagery that no one had ever seen in him; the deepest force of his dark nature emerged. With the voice of a lion he roared and bellowed for his children as if they had been taken away from him. His hand reached out for a powerful hammer lying nearby, and he swung it over his head. His brothers came dashing inside, but he seemed to know no one, not even them, seemed to recognize none of them but raved instead as if he thought they had murdered his children or hidden them away. His wife had risen up halfway on her knees, her whole body trembling as she gnawed at her hands in fear and humiliation. The hunchback bared his teeth in an ugly way and pressed himself against the wall; the one-eyed and one-armed brothers hid behind dyeing vats and barrels. The Dyer let out another mighty roar for his children. His brothers now began shouting at him, and the familiar sound of their ugly voices seemed to have made its way into his soul. He lowered the hammer, his expression grew calmer, and his eye no longer glared so menacingly in every direction. The Nurse was by his side in a flash; she took the hammer away from him and tossed it behind some barrels against the wall, busily jabbering the whole time. She reproached him for drinking some unknown liquid from a squat bottle, which made him thrash around the floor for an hour, act like a fool, and curse and swear like a wild man. Then she called on his own brothers as witnesses to behavior they could not have observed. The Dyer's Wife was looking at her breathlessly; soon she herself no longer knew what had in fact happened and what had not; nor did she want to know. She felt she was choking on her own blood. She looked blankly at Barak once more; her eyes were still full of fear, but their expression soon gave way to a sneer that contorted her appealing face. Barak was now standing there shamefaced; his brothers were all shouting at him with questions and reprimands as he bent down and began gathering up spilled grains of wheat, moving as if half-asleep. Some decision suddenly showed in his face. His expression grew easier. With utmost amazement, his brothers saw him kneel down in front of his wife and ask her forgiveness. His tone was humble but solemn: he asked her forgiveness for having been so foolish as to marry late in hopes of enjoying long life, children, and riches. He was trying to say something else, but he could not get it across his lips. The Dyer's Wife and the Nurse exchanged a single glance; cold insolence was written on the young woman's face, but her knees were still shaking as she yanked away the garment he had taken hold of. She did not answer him but said something to the Nurse about mules that make their way step by step along dizzying precipices without having it in them to be astounded or afraid. This man here, her husband, was just like them, and they were sterile as well. He turned to all of them as if to ask for forgiveness, but then he pointed to his wife.

"Words like these," he said, "must be forgiven; they relieve the soul; if not for them people would find it too hard to carry their burdens."

His brothers shrugged their shoulders, left him standing there, and went outside so they could grumble about how he let himself be saddled and bridled, over and over again, whenever his young wife pleased. Barak kept standing there the whole time, hesitant and ashamed. The Empress could not look at him; when his wife had snatched her garment out of his hands, she felt something split inside of her and something else enter her that made her whole soul tremble. Barak turned to go outside. Then he turned back once more, fixed his round eyes on the Nurse and the Empress, hesitated until the words came into his mouth, and finally said, "Her tongue is sharp"—nodding toward his wife—"and her temper peevish but not evil, and everything she utters is blessed with the blessing that it can be revoked for the sake of her pure heart and her youth; and I am happy that she is healthy once more," he added, addressing the other two with deep solemnity and an indescribable air of understanding, "for last evening she was sick." Then he went slowly and with head lowered to his work.

Chapter Six

The Dyer's Wife had thrown herself onto her bed and hidden her face. The Nurse was flattering and caressing her, but to no avail. The younger woman let it happen but took no notice.

"O mother of mine!" she cried out with a loud sigh. "O mother of mine," she then said to herself, "what kind of strength did you think I possessed when you charged me to love forever the man you steered my way? Where would you have found such strength to give me?" She softly whispered these words to herself; her lips were moving, but nothing could be heard. Suddenly she leapt to her feet. "Onward," she cried, "it is time for me to stop being a child!" Again, she seemed to be saying these words more to herself. She wrapped a shawl around herself and went toward the door.

"Where are you going, my mistress?" cried the Nurse. Only now did the Dyer's Wife seem aware she was not alone. She looked sternly and warily at the Nurse.

"It is time," she said, "for me to talk with my mother and untie my bonds, for she has burdened me with something I no longer wish to carry." She went out the door.

"Onward," the Nurse whispered, "because she will have need of us." The Empress moved off to the side; she would rather have moved quietly over to the Dyer, but the Nurse took her hand and led her along.

The Dyer's Wife was walking with quick, bold steps like a young mare inhaling the morning air, and the other two followed at a short distance. They crossed the river but did not make for the blacksmiths' quarter, turning right instead, where the ground rose, and followed a narrow, tumbledown street crowded with people. This was where the poorest of the poor lived—the tinkers, the rag-pickers, the trappers, huddled in thick tangles like rats. The Dyer's Wife stopped for a moment at a corner where this street crossed another just like it. She narrowed her eyes and looked into a court-yard teeming with men, women, and children; then she said to herself, "Look at that little child, so dirty they have to hold it out to the dog so he can lick it clean; yet it is as beautiful as the rising sun—and it is ones like these we are prepared to sacrifice." She said these words in a curious tone of voice, almost a singsong. They turned in but kept on going down-ward past a slope between ancient walls half fallen. This was one of the ravines that cut through the city here and there, its slopes not built up and still showing scant remains of dwell-ing places long since in ruins. Below it was a cistern lined by stones and next to it an old burial ground with a few trees. The Dyer's Wife walked up to her mother's grave; she threaded her way quickly among the gravestones, her feet not stirring up the dusty ground, her footsteps noiseless. She dropped to her knees, hands outstretched, before a small gravestone. She lowered her forehead to the stone; a twisted willow tree bent over her. She seemed to have become immersed in deep prayer with her very first breath. The sun was sinking behind her into a thick haze, as if into a crater. Everywhere among the graves, columns of dust swirled up silently and then sank down again like sacks. A gust of wind swept through, tearing away the last words from the lips of the Dyer's Wife. She rose abruptly, her movements like those of an animal whose whole bearing reveals no memory of the seconds just past. Her face no longer looked like itself; she was more beautiful than ever; her hair had come undone and was flying loose.

"Why are you looking at me like that?" she called out to the Nurse, who was observing her with delight. "I have now thrown off my yoke and crawled out from under an old law!" She quickly started up the slope, the Nurse on her heels. "It need not be near water; it can also take place by fire, can it not?" cried the Dyer's Wife over her shoulder. "That was what you said, my teacher! And I took special note of it." The wind swept down on all three of them and tugged at their garments as it stirred up the dust. It was dark in the middle of the day, as if night would come at any moment. Birds darted among the houses, people hurried past them in a brownish-red mist, and darkness came down from above, covering everything. When they came to the bridge, the Dyer's Wife all of a sudden began walking slower. She came to a stop and then took a few more steps. She stumbled as if she'd been struck a blow and brought a hand up to her head, near her ear. As she did, she stepped right in front of a wagon. The driver wrenched the animals back. Several of those passing by stopped in spite of their hurry.

"What is it that's assaulting you?" cried the Nurse as she sprang toward her. The young woman, now ice cold, fell into her arms at once.

"That voice!" she said in lament. "My mother's voice! It's in my ears. Don't you hear her?"

"What is she saying?" the old one asked.

"Barak!" groaned the Dyer's Wife. "She is calling out for him. She says he must bind me fast. She wants to hold me by my hands so he can kill me. She does not wish me to live so that I can do what I have resolved to do." Her face had turned completely gray, her eyes suffused with a bluish color. The Nurse reached for her hands, which were burning hot; suddenly the young woman tore herself loose and stormed away among all the people, the Nurse pursuing her. When the Empress caught up with her in a narrow street by the river bank, the Dyer's Wife was sitting on the ground, her back propped against a wall, and her breathing was rapid and shallow; the Nurse was squatting next to her. Several people had stopped to look at the woman lying there, a few old goodwives, a muleteer, and an old man. The Empress stepped directly into their midst; the muleteer shoved her half aside and then pressed against her, but she did not notice.

The Nurse hissed, "Away with you!" and covered the young woman with her dark mantle. They all went on their way until only a child was standing there.

"Water!" gasped the Dyer's Wife. The Nurse beckoned the child, who then held out a wooden bowl filled to the brim; it was as if she had snatched it out of the air. From the bowl wafted a gentle but troubling odor exactly like the one that had filled the room just before the ifrit appeared. The Dyer's Wife bent her head toward the bowl, which the Nurse was holding out to her. The child was no longer there.

"Drink this," said the Nurse, "and know that your mother speaks with forked tongue, even in her grave, and is a nasty shrew as well. Her words must simply be brushed aside, for it is the undesired ones who are speaking through her mouth."

A change came over the face of the Dyer's Wife as soon as she had drunk: a sudden glow mounted to her cheeks and her eyes were swimming like those of someone drunk. She got back up on her feet and flung her arm in a very peculiar motion around the Nurse's neck; they then turned back toward the bridge. The Empress made sure to keep close by them. They were speaking with great eagerness, but always directly into the other one's ear, so she could not make out anything they were saying.

As they came close to the Dyer's house, the three brothers leapt out of the darkness toward them, tore the young woman away from the other two, and began shouting at her, their faces contorted, "He is ordering us to bring him his children; he says they have been spirited away!" they cried out. "Where have you hidden them? What have you done to them? He is abusing and battering us, and it's because of you, accursed woman; he is taking it out on us, who know nothing of your furtive tricks and your wrongdoings!" The Dyer's Wife only wrinkled her brow, not deigning to reply to her brothers-in-law.

"What did you put in that drink, you witch?" the middle brother shouted, pushing at the Nurse's chest with his long arm. "He looks right at us but doesn't see us; instead he sees sitting at his table seven children who aren't there, and he greets them as his guests." The Dyer's Wife pulled herself free.

"Now we are about to find out if my words can be revoked!" she said and crossed the threshold. The Dyer was hunkered down in the ashes on the hearth. His tools were scattered before him in disarray; all his trowels and scoops, his ladles made of wood, pewter, and horn, large and small, as if children had tossed them all about as they played. With his large hands he was dipping hollyhock leaves with great care in the dirty water left over from dyeing that was now all over the floor; he had one leg in a scarlet-red puddle. The woman came to a stop in front on him; he took no notice of her. He was speaking to children who were not there.

"Hard-working children," he said, "spotless little hands," he added with a kindly nod. He was showing them how the work is supposed to be done. "We take the dyes from flowers and fix them in the cloth; others we take from insects and from the breast feathers of birds, glowing when uncovered." He was speaking slowly, giving instruction; his voice sounded indescribably happy.

His wife called out to him—"Barak!" He then listened, but not quite in the direction from which his name had been called; he turned more upward and sideways. Even so, he stood and went over to her. His powerful body, seemingly guided by no mind or spirit, came lurching toward her in so fearsome a way, especially since it was night, that she instinctively shrank back a pace. But she took control of herself, and her face, though pale, remained bold and resolute. "Barak, do you hear me?" she cried loudly in his face.

"Speak to us, brother and guardian," cried the one-eyed man. "She has poisoned you, our brother," shouted the hunchback in rage and pain, "and you will soon no longer be able to recognize those near and dear to you."

"Silence them, Barak," the woman said. "Do not let them keep on howling like dogs. For I have something I must say to you. I hear you speaking with those whom you believe will yet come. But now, at last, know this and take it to heart: they have been shunted away, because they wanted to do me an evil turn, and therefore they deserve to suffer what will befall them." Barak stepped closer to her; his eyes had grown blood-shot, and they were not protruding now but sitting deep in their sockets, and their expression was terrifying. "Look here," the woman said, "I can see you understand, so why aren't you saying anything? This is the last time the two of us will ever exchange breath."

"Light a fire," said Barak. His voice was unrecognizable, as if some complete stranger were speaking from inside him, but his brothers had their eyes trained on him the whole time and saw that it was his own mouth moving. The misshapen one threw himself to the floor quickly and blew on the ashes in the hearth; a flame leapt up, and the woman was standing all at once in the full glow of the fire, whose brightness danced up and down her figure; she was beautiful and malevolent beyond measure. She opened her mouth, and as her lips moved, scornful and yet forceful, her face below her disdainfully lowered eyelashes looked like an unbreachable fortress.

"You caused a fire to flare up, so now you can see me and look your fill at what you soon will never look upon again. But you must also understand that I would not have you become a laughingstock like some clumsy oaf who lets his bed be stolen out from underneath him." The Dyer stood in the dark without moving; only his upper body now leaned forward a little; his teeth could be seen, as could his eyes, glowing red. The woman only lowered her lashes farther and continued speaking in a voice that sounded like a string about to snap: "Look here and see that I am beautiful. My beauty is not for the likes of you, and that is why you have not been able to untie the knot in my heart. My beauty has called forth another, for it is a powerful magic." She could feel that she wanted to stop speaking, but the fierce determination in her heart compelled her to go on. "And therefore I have sealed a pact and shall yield up my shadow and the undesired ones along with it, and a price has been agreed on, which I now name to you: it is the smoothness of my cheeks forever and breasts that will never wither, so that those who come to hail me will tremble at the sight of them, and there is one who is the first among them, and from this moment on I belong to him." She tossed back her head and grew silent. A short burst of noise was forced out of Barak's lungs; it had almost no resemblance to a human sound, but it confirmed for all the rest that he had understood his wife's words.

"Quick," cried the Nurse and reached into thin air; in her blackened, claw-like hand she was holding out seven fish to the Dyer's Wife. They were strung along a willow twig by their gills, like keys on a ring. "Throw them over your head into the fire, and then let us be off. It is now time."

The Dyer's Wife pressed her lips together and reached for the fish.

"Away with you at once, and stay near my shadow!" the Nurse prompted her.

But Barak took a step toward his wife, and she shrank back. Her lips were moving, and she muttered the words, but it was as if she did not know she was doing so. She raised the hand that was holding the fish over her shoulder and threw them, but as if in sleep; she did what she had been directed to, though in such a way as if she weren't doing it at all. Her eyes remained fixed on the Dyer, and her lips were twisted like those of a child trying to cry out. "O mother of mine!" she called, her voice sounding like the voice of a five-year-old. She took a pair of hesitant steps but could not find help any-where, so she shut her mouth tight and came to a stop. The Dyer was right behind her now; in her fear she pulled herself together and dashed through the door like an arrow. He tried to go after her, but his brothers were holding him tight and shouting that he mustn't become a murderer! He shook the brothers off, and they went tumbling down onto the Nurse, who was squatting next to the fire and grabbing at the fish.

"Begone. Away, troublesome creatures!" she cried, tossing the fish into the fire. The one-eyed and one-armed brothers closed in on the witch; each had hauled a burning log out of the fire, but then they followed the third brother outside; the Nurse, after watching the fish sizzle in the fire, went dashing after the brothers. A storm was raging outside as though all the elements had been unleashed. The darkness roared and roiled, and thick clouds of dust surged through the impenetrable dusk; roof tiles came crashing down from the shed while at the same time the foaming river spilled over the bank and tore at the floating bridge so that it groaned and the iron chains by which it was suspended sounded as if they were about to tear loose.

The storm drove sparks into the two brothers' faces and caused the firebrands to burn so fiercely that they were soon holding nothing more than smoldering stubs; they had staggered away from the threshold and were crying out into the unknown for the Dyer. The Nurse saw his wife standing against the wall of the shed, the Empress close in front of her, motionless as a statue. The Dyer was standing about ten paces away from his wife; he was facing toward her and must have been able to see her or at least sense in spite of the darkness where she was standing. The hunchback was near him.

"Firebrands out!" shouted the Dyer in a voice that rang out over the storm and the groaning of the bridge and the creaking of the shed, as he pointed to his wife with outstretched arm. The glow from the fire was now coming from the house and revealing her to him as she cowered in fear.

The Nurse moved closer; no sight made her happier than seeing humans inflicting violence on one another.

"We have secured a right and now mean to enforce our claim!" she murmured to herself.

"Fetch that huge creel!" called the Dyer. The hunchback flung himself onto the bridge and untied the creel that was hanging in the water from a chain; as he was doing so, the water surged over him three times and almost washed him away. The Dyer bent down, and in the flickering light from the door it could be seen that he was groping with his hands for the millstone lying on the ground a few steps away. He lifted it and dropped it into the creel, which was large and flat enough that a person could be squeezed into it. There was a splash of water when the heavy stone fell. The hunchback now came running out of the house; he had tossed burning logs into a large flat bowl, so now a harsh light was falling over them.

"A rope!" cried the Dyer. The brothers understood what he was about to do, and they dropped to their knees.

"No blood on your hands, brother!" they cried as if with one voice. The saw the Dyer start toward his wife, and they turned their faces aside.

"Flee!" they bellowed to the Dyer's Wife, shooing her away with their long arms as they would an animal. "Begone with you, and may you meet with a dog's fate."

They bent down to pick up rocks; the hunchback was trying to throw a burning log at her but stumbled, and the bowl with the burning logs fell out of his hand into a tub lying nearby, so they were now all standing in a darkness too deep for them to see their hands. Only the Nurse, whose eyes, like those of a night bird, could pierce even the darkest gloom, saw the Dyer's Wife get up off her knees at that moment, gather her skirts together, and dart like a lightning bolt past the brothers and toward her husband. The Nurse leapt closer. She thought she could see the shadow of the Dyer's

Wife twitching itself loose, trying to get away from her to join company with other shadows; fluttering about here and there were scraps of dyed fabric that had torn loose from the drying stands and become stuck, while the looming shadows of the tubs and vats kept leaping up and shrinking back in the wavering darkness. Then it occurred to her that she had left the Empress out of her sight for a moment. She looked around, and the place where the Empress had been standing was empty. At the Dyer's feet a female figure was lying prostrate, its face pressed to the ground; with utter humility the woman now extended her arm, not showing her face, until she reached the Dyer's feet and embraced them. The Dyer seemed not to notice. His large, solid body was heaving in the darkness at regular intervals. The prostrate woman used her hands to slink closer, until her chin was resting on the dyer's feet. Her lips were murmuring words no one could hear. Then she came to rest as if she were dead. The Nurse peered intently, and when the logs in the bowl once more burst into flame, setting the wooden tub on fire as well, she saw that the woman lying there cast no shadow. She thought she had been cheated out of the shadow; shock and rage made her tongue dart back and forth in her toothless mouth, and she was about to leap to the prostrate woman's side when she sensed someone moving halfway behind her and saw the Dyer's Wife standing there, her hands outstretched toward her husband. She realized at once that the woman on the ground was the Empress and took such fright that she had to step up directly behind her. The face of the Dyer's Wife had taken on a beauty wonderful in its innocence; her terrible fear was not disfiguring her but transfiguring her instead. The Dyer took half a step toward her, still with that blank expression, like someone half in a dream; his movement made him jostle the head of the woman lying on his foot, but he did not notice. The torch flared up, and the young face opposite him, prepared for death as it was, shone out so brightly that he started back. Something came over his face that no one could see; it was as if inside him a blindfold had been torn from his eyes. His glance met that of his wife for just a flash, but each glimpse devoured the other in a way that had never happened before. He now saw something that all the caresses during his con-jugal nights, of which he and his wife had passed seven hun-dred, had never shown him, for those nights had always been sullen and blind. He saw a woman at once virgin and spouse whom no hands could touch, whom no embraces could hold, and the magnificence, the unfathomable depth of their glance smote him hard in the chest; he inhaled the pure air through his wide nostrils like a beast snorting in fear, and his mighty fists, now raised, began trembling. The impenetrable mys-tery of their glance seared away the impurities of his blood like lightning; even given the mass of his powerful body, he looked like a child about to cry.

She saw his powerful body looming up before her, the enormous power locked up inside him trying to burst forth from his eyes, his mouth, and his active limbs, and because that power was now, for once, not trying to overwhelm her like an avalanche, she was released from her spell and cast a clear, piercing look at him. To her, his power was like a lion's and his weakness like a child's. With affectionate fear she felt alarm at witnessing such extreme opposites, and she at once felt an impulse toward uniting this duality inside herself—her knees gave way for virgin-like fright, and her heart embraced that powerful man with maternal tenderness. Her mouth was filled with the pearls of unkissed kisses, and from her eyes there flashed like sparks of fire the rapture she was now able to receive and to give. At this moment she gave herself to him as she never had before—in an embrace without entanglements and a kiss in which their lips neither met nor separated.

At this moment they were truly man and wife; at this moment, too, heeding the magic spell and bound by obedience to the words that had been spoken and to the fish ritually offered—the last of them had at this very moment burned to glowing ash—the shadow detached itself from the back of the Dyer's Wife and quicker than any bird flitted across the ground toward the water, for flowing streams could attract it as much as glowing fires, and it was attempting to save itself from grasping hands and bondage to strangers.

"Here to me!" screamed the Nurse, bending over the water to grasp the shadow in her claws. "Come here and seize what is yours!" she called out of breath over her shoulder to the Empress.

At exactly that same moment the three brothers, standing behind her, cried out in one voice, shouting with utmost astonishment and horror: before their very eyes the Dyer and the Dyer's Wife had vanished. From the other side of the river a light was now moving toward those remaining; the Nurse opened her eyes wide, and she stared out at the approaching brightness without blinking even once. Her hair stood on end, and every nerve inside her tensed; it was the spirit messenger soaring so unexpectedly over the water, and the surface of the river had suddenly grown still and was reflecting the armor made of blue scales. His gleaming eye seemed to be searching her out as she stood rigidly waiting for him to come nearer. His cloak trailed behind him, and now he rose higher above the water and brushed past her in an arc; the shadow of the Dyer's Wife had affixed itself to his rippling cloak, and he soared away, the shadow on his cloak, without casting a single glance the Nurse's way.

"You! Up! At once! After him!" she screamed and was at the Empress's side in three leaps. "We must now take hold of that which we have labored to obtain as our right!"

The Empress lay there like a corpse, but when the Nurse gently lifted her head, she saw that her eyes were open. She cradled the Empress in her lap and spoke to her. And now the Empress turned her glance to the Nurse, but it looked into sheer vacancy in a way terrible to see; she seemed to recognize the Nurse, but her face filled with dread and she closed her eyes once more. It was unbearable to the Nurse to be looking at a face that now totally resembled the face of a mortal woman. She helped the stunned Empress up from the ground; her head lolled backwards over the Nurse's arm. The older one wrapped her dark cloak around them both, enfolded her charge with both arms, and they set off through the darkness. The Nurse knew exactly what road she had to take.

CHAPTER SEVEN

Along the river, hemmed in here by the smooth, sheer cliffs of the Mountains of the Moon, yet flowing very fast with no swirls or eddies, a skiff was moving deeper into the mountain range, for that was the direction of the current. It found its way with no steersman; the Nurse, seated aft on the planking, seemed to be guiding it by her watchful glance, which she kept fixed on the fast-flowing water, looking out past the prow all the while by the length of an arrow's flight. The Empress was lying at her feet asleep.

The cliffs gradually began to recede. Tall trees, all beautiful, all of different kinds, and scattered as if on rich pastureland or a broad meadow stood left and right on the banks. Behind them rose the black and gleaming walls of rock on whose dark, mighty mass the whole expanse of Keikobad's hidden fastness was built. The Nurse could see moving among the trees a number of the messengers whose coming each month she had always carefully concealed from her charge. She recognized with repugnance the old one, whose white form had one night, just as the first month was over, stepped out from a wall on the staircase of the blue palace and had frightened her with his intense, forbidding gaze. She also saw the fisherman walking at a distance; he was again wearing, as before, a kind of short cloak woven of reeds, and in his hands were his nets, on which the water glistened. His red-gold hair was tied up in back like a woman's. But no one was paying the skiff and the new arrivals any heed, so the Nurse remained calm. It was by her will that the mantle, wrapped inside which they had both flown through the air, had set itself down in the region close to the moon mountains, near the bank of the river, a place she trekked through with assurance but through which no mortal would ever find a way if not guided; it was none of her doing, however, that the mantle had instantly turned into a skiff large enough to hold her and the unconscious woman with her, and she was now transporting her mistress to the place to which she had so longed for them to return. She felt how Keikobad's command was holding sway in all things, so he must no longer be implacably wrathful towards them; she was aware that she had served her mistress to the letter and duped the mortals, every one of whom she found loathsome. All her dealings appeared to her in a good light; she was happy and prepared to receive her reward. She only wondered why she wasn't seeing the messenger in the blue armor; she was resolved to confront him face to face and heap shame upon him, for she felt the law of the spirit world to be on her side. Still, she could not forget the last look the Empress had given her when she had raised her mistress up from the dark ground by the wall of the Dyer's house. That look, one whose meaning she could not fathom, was terrible to her in its blend of despairing dread and chilling rebuke. And to her it was as if she had never even seen the Empress lying at the feet of a mortal man. She leaned overboard and washed her eyes and cheeks with the clear, dark water, scooping it with both hands; then she rubbed her neck and her throat clean of the magical fluid, which left no traces on her hands. Now she felt the skiff shifting direction, as if it were being towed by a rope from the bank. Hardly had she turned than she saw the one in the blue armor standing atop a flat rock on the bank; he seemed to have been expecting the skiff. Now he receded into the trees. She could now see only his back; he wore his blue-black hair in a braid hanging down his neck; his cloak was tossed over the armor and hung short; even though stocky in build, he made an appearance both comely and commanding. Even as she kept peering after him, he had already vanished among the trunks of the trees. The skiff gently put in at the river bank at the same time, while the Empress had by now tossed aside sleep and stepped onto solid ground as lightly as a bird alighting. Her gray outer garment, in which she had covered herself when among mortals, had dropped away and remained in the skiff; she was now wearing only a thin, snow-white garment wrapped fast around her limbs. No one would ever have imagined it was there under the gray covering. With just one look she recognized where she was; she had often been here in the shape of a young snake, and as a bird she had hovered in the air over the bushes and the water here. None of that entered into her now, however. Her look changed at once; her shining eyes turned dark and angry.

"Where am I?" she asked and gave the skiff below her a hard kick. "Where have you brought me while I was asleep and knew nothing of myself! Where is the man? Where is the woman? I must be off, must again kneel at their feet so I can make amends to them!"

The face of the Nurse underwent a transformation out of sheer astonishment at these words. She could comprehend nothing of what was so compelling to the Empress. In washing her face, she had also washed away the last memory of those two mortals and their paltry house; by now she had completely forgotten what the Dyer and his wife looked like.

"Who are those of whom you are speaking?" she called up from below. "How could they ever be worth the breath you're wasting on them?" Then she turned her head away. She had noticed the fisherman now stepping out from the bushes on the opposite bank. She was not pleased at feeling his glance on the skiff and on her. Even now she recalled how harshly he had treated her after being dispatched at the end of the seventh month to find out if the spirit child were yet casting a shadow. He had come up to her from behind as she was walking along the edge of the pool behind the blue palace, tossed his net over her, and drawn her to himself in the water. She knew he might do the same again now, but the fury of her mistress had more power over her than her misgivings about the messenger. She had never been able to grasp that this great one, standing unapproachably high above her and trembling with rage like a flame wreathed in white smoke, had lain on the dark, damp ground at the feet of a mortal.

"Away with us, and you first," cried the Empress, "find them for me once more, even if they have been snatched away by spirits and taken a thousand leagues from their dwelling. For we have incurred the guilt of robbing and murdering them, and all the blood in our veins is too little to make good what we have done to them."

The Nurse cowered to the side, unable to bear her mistress's look; to her it was as if the Empress were about to swoop down on her from above and strike out at her with the heels of her gleaming feet, so fearsome was the rage in her features. From the corner of her eye, however, she could at the same time see over the edge of the skiff; she caught sight of how the fisherman stepped so close to the edge of the opposite bank that the water swirled at his feet, how he stretched out his arm commandingly and signaled her to bring him across with the skiff. At once she felt the craft heed the signal on its own and move away from the bank.

"Here! Come to me!" she shouted to the Empress, because she understood in a flash that they were intending to separate her from her charge. But the Empress gave no answer. She had both arms pressed against her bosom and was holding her head high, though her eyes were closed. The Nurse clung to a tree root on the bank, but it was too late, for the skiff pulled her away and across. The fisherman had leapt in by now, tossed away his nets, and flung the old woman down so that she fell onto one of them. In the middle of the stream he steered the skiff downstream; gnashing her teeth, she saw high walls of rock closing in like a huge portal on both sides and the skiff go sailing through them. The Empress had vanished from her sight. Hunched on the net, still soaked, the old woman pondered how she might bring the craft under her control once more, how she might find a way of turning it back, which she had now greater need of than ever. The fisherman was paying her no need; he pushed up his sleeves, reached deep into the water, and drew out a willow basket long and slender in shape, like a large scabbard. Not a single drop of water clung to the basket; it was as if he had plucked it from above, out of the shining air. The skiff had meantime started moving more slowly, now gliding toward a gently sloping bank and coming to a stop between willows and alders. The fisherman put the basket under his arm, threw his nets across his shoulders, and stepped onto the shore. He followed a path leading inland among the alders. She thought about quickly untying the skiff from the bank, but to her astonishment the fisherman had coiled the rope around an old willow stump and tied it into a knot she found impossible to undo; she could not understand how he had managed to accomplish that, quick as lightning, while disembarking.

Snarling with rage, she drew the Empress's garment around her and skulked along behind the fisherman, for she knew that the river twisted its way through the moon mountains like an S, and she knew of a narrow, dangerous place higher up where she had once been able to swing by an overhanging tree to a cliff across the chasm; she was now hoping to reach this place by cutting across the mountainous terrain. She had not gone far along the ascending footpath when she saw the fisherman's hut lying among birches and hazel bushes; blue smoke was rising from it. She crept to the window and looked in. In one corner of the single half-dark room a young woman, whose limbs looked fragile, was lying on a pallet of reeds in restless sleep. Kneeling at her feet was the fisherman's wife, gray-haired but with a face rather young still, so that she seemed just about equal to her husband in age. She was absorbed in watching the sleeping woman's hands, which she was wringing and then drawing apart again in some fiercely oppressive dream that now weighed on her very heavily. The Nurse had known the elder of the two women all her life, but she had never found any liking for her. The fisherman's wife was eager beyond measure to pry and was incapable of keeping anything to herself. She possessed little courage or strength of will, but she had the ability to see whatever was hidden by walls, containers, or draperies, could find meaning in symbols and signs of every kind, knew how to discern from the faintest of traces much that remained concealed from others. Living secluded from people as she did, she was filled with joy that the young woman had been entrusted to her care. Just now, as the sleeping woman moved her head at the entrance of the fisherman, the Nurse recognized her as the Dyer's Wife, whom she had never expected to see again, and there escaped from her an angry sound of surprise, one she half managed to stifle in her throat. On the lips of the fisherman's wife were a thousand questions.

"Why did you not tell me," she flung at the man walking in, "that among mortals there are such as cast no shadow, not even, as it befell an hour ago, when the sun was shining slantwise through the window? And what wrong has this woman done that she is now so deeply fearful? For she is bold and unrestrained, as I see by her hands, and a dreamer, and her heart is pure, though the plaything of her desires and her dreams. And," she interrupted herself here, "what is that basket you have brought with you, and what understanding am I to have of the being that has crept along behind you and now is lurking about behind our house – neither mortal nor yet beast, but somehow of our own kind?" So saying, she raised her head and sniffed the air. As was his habit, the fisherman gave her no answer; he spread out his nets instead. His wife had already drawn closer to the basket, however, and by penetrating the tight weft of wicker with her eyes, she answered one of her questions herself.

"A sword of judgment and a blood-red carpet!" she cried half aloud. "Is the carpet for her knees and the sword for her neck?" she whispered, pointing to the sleeping woman, who shuddered as if she had heard those words. "Who will sit in judgment?" the wife asked. "And is she meant to carry the basket on her head to the place of execution? Is it for this reason you have brought it here?" She stopped looking at the hands of the Dyer's Wife and turned her gaze to the younger woman's lips, which were moving almost imperceptibly. "How staunch yet submissive she is!" the older woman exclaimed. "'Let me die before the sun is up,' she is saying. 'Only set no torch alight. The sword will flash anyway, and the carpet will gleam with all the blood it has drunk, but no one will see that I cast no shadow.' To whom is she speaking these words?" the fisherman's wife with eager curiosity asked her husband, who had sat down on the chopping block and begun mending one of the nets. "Ah," she said, moving closer to the sleeping woman, "now she is praying and meekly kissing a man's hand, large and blue-black. 'Let come to pass with me whatever you will,' she is saying, 'for you are my judge, and I now kneel between your hands. But know that in the last hour of my life I saw you for who you are and know that you untied the knot of my heart.' But who is it that will be her judge? Answer me! I am alone the livelong day, and when I am at last given a strange being for company, it is a woman asleep, one who does not open her mouth. Who shall sit in judgment upon the creature lying here?"

"The golden water!" answered the man.

"The water of life?" cried the woman in an astonished voice. "No one even told me that it had come back into the mountain. Can it speak, then, and pronounce a sentence?"

"No, but it can transform, and that is more."

"Transform? Change shapes? That is a gift like any other," she retorted. "Does not the old one, your stepbrother, trans-form into beasts that do his bidding everything menacing that comes toward him? And is it not given to you, furthermore, when you plunge your arms into water, to fetch forth what no one ever placed there?"

"Yes, but the golden water transforms that which cannot be seen," said the man.

"Someone is at the window," the woman whispered as she rose quick as a flash from the ground. The fisherman stepped over to the sleeping woman and observed how she sighed in her sleep, as though her heart would burst, while tears flowed from under her eyelashes and ran down her cheeks.

Even as the fisherman's wife was making her way outside, the Nurse was up and gone. Her mood was almost worse than a year before, when she had lost the fairy child and did not know how to find any trace of her. The presence of the young woman here in the spirit realm filled her with some indefinite, stifling fear. She was hastening onward and upward. Now she was surrounded by nothing but rocks, among which it was no longer easy for even a being with her gifts to find her way. Yet she still knew where she was.

Not far from here there had to be a chasm in which, trudging laboriously the year before in search of the lost child, she had found tolerable shelter for the first night. Now she recognized the narrow, deep-cut ravine; out of it there came a lynx, waiting and looking expectantly backwards, like a dog for its master. At the same time she saw the white-garbed old one emerging as well, at his side a lamb looking up at him with an air of wisdom. And in the tall man who was now stepping out from inside the mountain—slowly and feet wide apart, a man for whom the old one waited and to whom, like a guide leading a guest unaccustomed to mountain paths, he was respectfully pointing out the solidly placed flagstones on which to set his powerful foot—she recognized the Dyer, and she was filled with terror. She felt as if a net were being drawn tight about her from far off, a net whose mesh she would not be able to rip apart. She had climbed high, off to the side, among tree roots and bare rocks; hanging over them, she could hear what the two were saying to each other.

"When will I see her again?" the Dyer asked, as a powerful sigh heaved out of his chest.

"When the sun above the river is mounting upward," answered the old one.

They went on talking, and once again a mention of the golden water struck her ear. From childhood on, an awed fear of this powerful magic had been instilled in her; she wanted to hear those words no more, so she crawled from tree to tree, from slab to slab. She thought she had an inner sense of her bearings, but the chasm grew ever wilder and the trees now stopped. Her listening was in vain. The river flowed soundlessly far below, there was no sign or mark to be found, and she had to admit to herself that she had lost her way. She cried out her child's name, loud and shrill, but there came no answer, not so much as an echo. Only a night bird flew out on soft wings from among the rocks, thudded against her body, and plunged to earth. She threw herself onto the ground and pressed her face against hard stone.

Meanwhile, the Empress was standing by herself among trees and rocks, behind which, off to her side, the light began to fade. Every object now cast a long shadow across the green forest floor; she and she alone cast none. She had turned to face the rock wall, believing she recognized the place; it was her clearest memory yet of an earlier time. Here is where her father had stepped forth with her; here is where he had quietly revealed to her the secret of transformation; she had felt herself changed into a bird for the first time, felt herself soaring upward before her father's eyes. She could not remember very much about what he looked like. He wore no crown, but his brow itself gleamed like a diadem—so much she still vaguely recalled.

"Father," she cried out fervently, "Father, where are you?" Her words died away.

It seemed to her that she was locked inside her own body like a captive. Instinctively she reached for the talisman. Piercing her like a blinding light was the memory of how and when the power of transformation had been taken from her, and he who had punished her in this way was now closer to her than ever. She could feel him now in his unapproachability, and some reflection from him now gleamed on her brow.

Behind her the Empress heard a splashing sound, as if someone had swung up onto the bank from the water. A shiver ran down her spine, for she suddenly knew she was no longer alone, and she turned around abruptly. A tall young boy was standing there between her and the water, stalwart and strong. She could well have thought it was the Dyer she saw there before her: feet planted far apart, brow furrowed, hair curly black. He wore a garment wondrous blue in color not as if someone had immersed a bolt of white cloth in the dyeing vat and blended the strengths of indigo and woad, but more as if the blue of the sea floor itself had been hauled forth and draped around his body. He remained fixed where he was and bowed low to her, his arms crossed over his chest. Then he looked all around in a circle, as though he might be afraid some witness would hear what he was about to say; he nodded his head with deliberation toward the river.

"Keep the woman away!" he cried.

Meanwhile, his garment had undergone a change; it now resembled the blue-black of deep night before the first of the sun's rays brighten the sky. Before the Empress could answer him, another being was there before her eyes. Had it stepped out from among the trees? Had it come forth from the earth? There it stood. It was a little girl, and from her feet, as dainty as if they were formed of wax, to her hair, deeply glimmering like copper, she resembled the Dyer's Wife.

The very moment she appeared, she opened her mouth and called in a clear, imperious voice, "Go and take your place among those of your own kind!"

But at the same time, as if seized by impatience, she came closer to the Empress, not by walking but by gliding on the green earth as if on glass, her feet together, and no other way of moving could better have matched the delicacy of her limbs and the radiant colors that suffused her form. Behind her, moreover, there now emerged another girl, much older than she, taller and more powerful by far than the one who had appeared first. She stood there silently, fixing a look like that of an animal upon the Empress; three little boys were clinging to her, and the girl glided backwards to her, all four pressed against their older sister. The Empress could not turn her glance away for a second at how the girl held the children close, with gentle hands and anxious looks, like a bird with her fledglings; her goodness was like the Dyer's goodness, but when she looked over to the Empress with a decisive but reserved glance, it was with the glance of the Dyer's Wife. She was a wondrous commingling of both, but with no feature of either; a fusion of the two instead. The Empress could feel her heart pounding, so drawn was she to these beings, but then the girl was off and gone. The brother was now standing there alone; he seemed to be waiting for the Empress to address him.

"Have you brought me a message?" she cried, smiling at him. His garment glowed forth, deep and dark, from violet into red. The color seemed to be coming toward him from some eternal realm, likewise the answers that rose up so slowly within him until they hesitantly reached the edge of his lips.

"We summon no one; we convey nothing. Our showing ourselves, woman, is all that is vouchsafed to us."

"Where is the other one?" the Empress asked; her glance moved longingly to the trees among which the girl had been standing.

"Here and not here, woman, as it may please you!" he said and rose up tall from his slightly bowed position; his might was rooted to the ground by his powerful feet, and his garment was now like blood being turned into gold; the trees gained reassurance of their lives, as from the first radiance of the rising sun.

"Is there a third?" the Empress asked.

"The mingling of the two," came from the boy's lips. "Where does that occur?"

"In the decisive moment." The Empress took a step toward him. "Lead me to those of whom you have knowledge," she said.

"We are not those who will lead you; others will," he said in answer.

"Then bring her to me!" cried the Empress.

The boy looked at her with flashing eyes, those of the Dyer's Wife, though the glance was the Dyer's. With gentle severity he lifted his hand toward her, resembling that other one, his father, as a reflection in a mirror resembles the person reflected; for it seemed as if maxims of wisdom and understanding were mounting up within him but were incapable of passing beyond his heavy lips, unburdening themselves instead in the gestures of his arms and the wise renunciation of his half-raised shoulders. The color of his garment sank from red into violet and resembled a cloud in the dark night sky.

"It is not we who are being brought before you, woman, but you who are being brought before us, and the hour is at hand." The Empress took a step back.

"Who is to sit in judgment on me?" she asked softly.

"The invisible ones are gathered, woman, may it please you!" he said and solemnly bowed to her; he could not have pronounced a death sentence with any greater solemnity. His garment was dark once more, like the night sky without stars. The Empress heaved a deep breath.

"I have transgressed!" she said.

She lowered her eyes but then at once raised them back up to him who was speaking to her. That being heeded carefully and did not answer right away. His very soul mounted into his eyes; he seemed to be caressing the words that came out of her mouth.

"So must all those say who set one foot in front of the other. That is why we walk with our feet together."

A hint of a smile hovered in his voice as he said that to her, but his face remained solemn, and in nothing did he resemble the Dyer more than in this profound somberness of his features.

"Can I undo what has happened?" cried the Empress.

Her eyes were fixed on his mouth, her awe of the one speaking to her in this way no less than his of her.

"The golden water alone knows what has and has not happened," he replied.

"Is it subject to my father?" she asked.

"The strongest forces love one another," said this being briefly.

It was as if a shadow of impatience were flitting across his powerful face.

"Are you not permitted to tell me more?" she cried.

"Let me answer!" a clear voice rang out.

At once one of the little boys was before her, and then again at once a second one beside him. The first one, the one so eager to reply, resembled the Dyer's youngest brother with his thin mouth and high, narrow brow. But then again he did not resemble him either, because his limbs and his back were straight, and instead of the shabby garb of the hunchback he was clothed in raiment of magnificent colors that looked like feathers plucked from the breast of a bird of paradise. The second one stretched out toward her an arm disproportionately long, like that of the one-armed man, and he fixed on her the Dyer's round eyes, while his alluring mouth, which was also demanding to speak, trembled in an enchanting way, like the mouth of the Dyer's Wife. The colors in which he was clad were indescribable; he looked like a bouquet of flowers in the early morning.

"Note this, O woman," cried the first one, "all our mother's words are spoken inside of time, and thus they can be revoked,"—

"but yours," the second one joined in, "yours will be uttered in a particular moment and so there will be no revoking them: thus has your fate been decreed."

"What do you mean?" cried the Empress. "What moment?"

"The only one possible," cried the little girl, ablaze as she drew near.

"What must I do?" asked the Empress, breathlessly keeping her eyes fixed on the three children.

"Everything is in that moment: the need and the deed!"

came a cry from a small, wide mouth, one that looked as if carved from the Dyer's mouth, over a broad body around which a coral-red apron was fluttering and under a tangle of black hair as think as a bush. The fourth child had flown down among the other three, and now they had their arms around one another's hips and shoulders. As they stood there smiling they resembled, in the bright colors of their garments and in the sparkle from their eyes, which they would first lower and then raise, a blooming hedge in which dark-eyed birds were nesting. They swayed back and forth before the Empress in a kind of silent dance like a hedge in the evening wind.

"Who is it that is my own kind?" the Empress asked quickly, for she saw how these beings were drifting apart and were threatening to vanish with a mischievous smile.

"We are, woman, to be sure, as are those with whom we are one!" they cried, and then they were gone more quickly than the blink of an eye.

"O let me see you once more!" the Empress called out, fixing her glance in yearning expectancy on the spot where the tall girl had been standing. She had not yet spoken those words out loud when the tall girl was standing there again, over by the trees now, as the smaller ones glided to her bosom and her hips and crouched at her knees as at a mother's knees.

A wind like a long-drawn breath now came forth from the mountain, and the leaves began to tremble strongly. The mild air between the trees and the river turned cool and damp, as in a burial vault. There now coursed through the bodies of all the children a fear so great that the Empress grew as frightened in her inmost being as they seemed to be. The tall girl leaned over, pressing the children to herself and covering them with her body. Filled with fear, she cast looks in all directions; as though her hands had doubled, she reached out and held all the children at the same time. But they were vanishing from her grasp. With dying expressions they hung onto her; then they underwent a fearsome disintegration, dissolving into thin air like a fog of different colors now swirling around her body. The fair girl's face had fallen in and was now tinged with foul gray shadows of death; her eyes, as though from the beyond, looked into the eyes of the Empress, whose heart swelled with a dull ache so that she had to press both hands over it. Now the brother took his mantle, black as night, and covered his sister's vanishing features, which as they were dissipating resembled the true face of the Dyer's Wife as never before. His face, likewise, now grown older and graver, looked exactly like the Dyer's as he drew his mantle over his head and wrapped himself in it.

"Will I see you again?" cried the Empress; feelings of guilt burdened her heart with chains, and she felt herself forged to those into whose existence she had entered unbidden. The one wrapped in his mantle pointed silently toward the mountain. She closed her eyes.

When she opened them again, the figures were gone; a bluish glow lightened the dusk among the tree trunks. The messenger was standing there. She was still bereft of her senses; she saw him without seeing him. He waited and made a stately bow to the Empress. Then at once he turned away, gesturing toward her, and stepped into the wall of rock; the Empress followed him. Their path took several turnings, and only the bluish reflection off the smooth walls showed her the way. All at once she saw the reflection and the figure at her side vanish: when she reached the appointed place, there was nothing. But she became aware of some other luminosity ahead, and she walked toward it. She was standing in a high round space; the stone wall closed behind her. High overhead a torch was set in a metal ring; it cast a strong light and gave off a wonderful aroma as it burned. Nothing else was in that round space but a low bench all around it, made of stone and gleaming darkly. The Empress saw that what she had been led to was a pool, one more beautiful and more splendid than even the most luxurious bathing places in her own palace. She lost herself, if only for a moment, in her feeling of unexpected and mysterious loneliness and in contemplation of the wondrous basin at whose edge she was standing. It looked like the same kind of rock out of which the walls were hewn, and from time to time it would glint with a light coming not from glistening veins but more a diffused flashing throughout the whole pool, like heat lightning in a dense and shapeless cloud mass. So it was not without fear that the Empress would have put her foot into the water. Yet at the same time a heavenly well-being came over her, as if penetrating her every limb along with the fragrance from the torch. She lowered herself to the edge of the pool, timidly and expectantly, like a bride. Her beloved had to be very nearby somehow; he had to be closer to her than she knew. He had always come to her, but now she was coming to him in this chosen place. When she thought that, an "ah!" passed her lips, bashful but yearning at the same time, and the breath that had become a sound caused her to blush from head to toe. Her limbs went slack, and she stretched her arms out toward the pool; the ground began swirling back and forth under her feet like a murky fog lit from below, as a swell of water, muted gold in color, suddenly surged upward and just as suddenly dropped back with a dark sound like doves cooing. She felt an urge to plunge into the dark gleam of this surging and receding as into a loving glance.

"Higher, higher!" she cried; the golden water surged up in a mighty jet, and the column, gleaming when the light from the torch touched it, gave out a swelling sound that almost broke her heart in two with its sweetness. Now the jet subsided once more and became a radiant flat surface; it filled the pool, and a golden haze played over it. In its midst the core of gloom pulled upward by the column of water was lying still; there it seemed as weighty as a bronze grave marker built into the middle of the pool. Reposing on a dark rectangular stone base was the statue; it had been stripped of all its weapons and was now wearing only light hunting armor, more as if an adornment, and even the silver-scaled greaves that might have protected him from a boar's tusk or a lynx's teeth were absent, the statue's legs bare and completely like marble, as were also the shoulders and the neck, from which the cloak had fallen away.

The Empress let out a scream and flung herself headlong into the golden basin, gently rippling; like a swan with outspread wings she darted toward her beloved. She bent over him but did not dare to kiss him. He lay beneath her, quiet and inexpressibly beautiful, but also inexpressibly strange. Everything about him was there—the man and the youth, the prince, the huntsman, the lover, the spouse—and nothing was there. She leaned over him with no idea how long; she did not move. She resembled a statue herself, a figure on a tombstone. Her breathing did not move her torso; her eye did not reveal what she was feeling; two crystal tears fell.

The torch burned ever brighter, drawing into itself the golden mist that rose up from the water. Soon it had dispelled the mist, and the golden water was now playing around the Empress's heels only, though contact with it did not wet her.

Then it was gone entirely. Half-unconsciously the Empress felt timid in the presence of the light above her, as if in the presence of a living being; she wrapped her cloak closer and tried to cover both herself and the Emperor with it—tried by lifting her arm, but she could not. Because she was so close, something entered into her from the statue; it was not coolness, and it was not coldness, but a feeling of inaccessible distance, like an abyss that has opened up, but into the infinite—the closer the farther. Now the statue rose up, slowly and peculiarly, in a way that her beloved had never risen after waking in their bed. He propped himself up on one arm, and his eyes opened with great effort. His glance met the rigid, fearful glance facing him; alien and frightful, it swept past the Empress. It brushed past her as he turned and looked over his shoulder toward the torch. Under the statue's terrifying glance there poured out onto one side of the round chamber more and more of the golden light streaming from the torch, while on the other a brownish dusk was spreading, into which the seated statue's sharp-edged shadow was falling.

The statue now gazed for a time at its own shadow and then slowly turned its head to where the Empress was standing; it was looking for the Empress's shadow. She shrank back and stood between the light and the wall; yet she could clearly feel that the wall behind her was shining in all the fullness of the light, stronger than anywhere else. When she took notice to the statue's eyes, she saw that they had widened. Its facial expression, stamped by appalling strain, was menacing even though not alive. It seemed as though at any second a ghastly scream would be forced from its petrified breast and shatter it. The Empress could no longer bear the sight; feeling faint, she turned her head despairingly aside. Now, as if a spirit messenger were approaching, a gleam of bluish light began emerging from the wall at exactly the spot by which she had entered; a shadow stepped forth and skimmed toward her. Now it sank to her feet; an unrecognizable face bent downward and grazed her knee, as if with a breath. She shuddered, knowing that this was the shadow of the strange woman that had devolved to her. The shadow's arms reached upward to her, the hands with their palms turned out; it was the gesture of a slave that is yielding itself completely as a matter of life or death. This kneeling creature was quivering like aspen leaves as it reached up, and the Empress herself was trembling through her whole being. Its hands joined, and on it was resting a round bowl with golden water. The shadow raised its arms higher and tremulously offered her the bowl, and itself along with the bowl. The Emperor had now risen almost completely and was leaning on his left arm only; he had stretched out his right in unutterable yearning and apprehension. His eyes remained fixed on his wife's hand with an expression in which hope and desperation were entwined like fighting serpents. The Empress bent her arm and took hold of the bowl without realizing it. He followed her movement with so much bliss that his face was transformed like a lover's in the throes of rapture. She could feel that she was losing her senses and would then drink. But however intently her glance was fixed on the liquid fire so close to her lips, she could still see from the corner of her eye that the wall had once more opened behind her, opposite from the place where the shadow had emerged, and that a veiled figure was standing to her rear. A garment flowed downward, darker than the starless sky at midnight; the figure standing there did not move a muscle. She saw him without seeing him, and she felt in the depth of her very entrails that this figure, when it cast off its covering, would reveal the features of Barak the Dyer, over the innocent threshold of whose house she had stepped unbidden three days before, and would turn his eyes toward her, reflected in the face of his oldest unborn son. She clutched the bowl against herself and felt the talisman at her breast under her garment move; dreadful and strange, as if spoken by one deep in sleep, the words of the curse mounted from her innermost self into her ear: "To stone for all eternity the hand that undoes this binding, unless it avert that fate by obtaining a shadow from the earth; to stone the body that hand belongs to." She could hear her own heart beating slowly and heavily as if it were that of a stranger. With a single glance, as though she were hovering outside her own being, she saw herself standing there, at her feet the shadow of the strange woman who had devolved to her, the statue beyond them. The terrible feeling of reality bound everything together as with iron bands. Coldness drifted her way, penetrating so deep that it numbed her. She could not move a step, neither forwards nor backwards. All she could do was take one of two actions: drink and gain the shadow or pour the water out of the bowl. She thought she was being annihilated and shrank down deep into herself; out of her diamond-hard depths there arose words inside her, distinct, as if they were being sung very far away; she had only to repeat them. And so she spoke them with no hesitancy.

"Barak, I am guilty of harming you!" she said, extending straight out the arm with the bowl and pouring out its contents at the feet of the veiled figure. The golden water flamed out in the air, the bowl in her hand vanished into nothingness, everything that had filled the room was gone, and the statue lay all alone like tarnished bronze on the black rock as the torch above them burned fiercely. From under them a shaking started, a mighty roaring of rising and surging waters. The torrent swept upward, engulfing the Empress and thrusting her aloft. The torch had gone toppling into the golden water and was now penetrating the darkly shining gloom with its light; by turns, radiant brightness and deep night flooded across the Empress's face. She felt herself rising higher and higher, and something dark was rising next to her. It was the statue, irresistibly driven upward just as fast as her light frame. Now she was lying cheek by jowl with the statue; its stone arms clasped themselves around her; a glance from the stone eyes met hers from very close, and it was heart-rending enough to soften a stone heart. The terrible burden kept clinging to her; then she wrapped her arms around the stone, entwining him completely. The climbing stopped, and she felt she was being hurled into an abyss. The smooth fearsome alien nature of the stone pierced her to her depths. Her senses were being shattered by inconceivable agony. She felt death creeping over her own heart but felt the statue coming alive at the same time. In her inconceivable state she surrendered to what was taking place inside her and could no longer do anything but tremble at some inkling of the life the other one was absorbing from her. There penetrated into him—or into her—a feeling of darkness that was growing lighter, of a great good place to welcome them, of swaying trees, of gentle, solid ground on which men and women could lie at rest, of the breadth of a brilliant sky. The river was sparkling in the distance and the sun rose from behind a hill, its rays shining onto the Emperor's face as he lay at his wife's feet, clinging to her knee like a child.

His eyelids twitched under the strong light breaking through the canopy of trees. The Empress stood up carefully and stepped between her slumbering beloved and the sun. She bent protectively over his sleep, like a mother, looking down on him with a gaze deep and silent. She had now grown aware with delighted astonishment that there was nothing about her husband's lithe figure, as he lay there breathing easily, to remind her of that terrifying statue. Inexpressible happiness now seized her, and a cry burst forth from her lips, for she saw a black shadow flow out from her across the body of the man lying before her and across the forest floor. Her outcry caused the Emperor to open his eyes; inexhaustible vitality was in his youthful glance, yet in its very deepest depths there still dwelt as the dark radiance of early wisdom the death he had undergone. She lifted him up toward her, and they embraced without a word as each of their shadows flowed into one.

Below them the skiff lay at a sheltered spot along the bank, as if waiting for the ferryman and a passenger. Just then, figures could be seen approaching the river by either bank; one group, consisting of two people, was moving slowly; the other, at a quicker pace, a man and two women, one of whom was carrying an oval-shaped basket on her head. The sunlight was shining on all five. The woman carrying the basket cast no shadow on the dew-pearled meadow they were crossing; her garments were as ashen as her face and her gait unsteady.

"Look! My falcon! Look, he is here too!" cried the Emperor, who took no notice of the surroundings and the figures, so ecstatically were his eyes completely fixed on the gleaming vault of the sky, where that wondrous bird was circling high above the mountain crest in its reddish radiance. A waterfall was sparkling below him. Among the dark boulders and the tall, dark tree trunks was hovering a blue-tinged light from the interior of the mountain. The spirit messenger drifted downward along the steep mountain wall, and then something dark wrenched itself free from under his feet und scurried as quick as lightning toward the bank and across the river. The shadow of the Dyer's Wife darted towards its mistress and fell at her feet. She did not know what it was that had dropped down so heavily; her heart, though now willing to yield completely, was able at this point to apprehend nothing except in the most dreamlike way. She stumbled, and the fisherman's wife, who was walking beside her, had to support her. The basket swayed on the woman's head. Its outline blurred as if amid blackish fumes; from it the sword was gleaming and the blood glinting by turns, but then it all dissolved into a marvelous play of colors, as if a rainbow had been compressed into the basket. The colors, bright as flames, drifted downward to the Dyer's Wife—tenderest green, fiery yellow, violet, and purple. They played across her body, revealing the full glory of the sun, and then vanished inside the woman faster than words can say. The fisherman's wife clapped her hands for sheer amazement. The Dyer's Wife stood in a blaze of color, arrayed like a queen of the sea. The color of life itself was now mounting into her face, her eyes gleaming like those of the young doe across the river. She was not looking down toward the ground and thus was not aware that her shadow had returned to her. From the other bank the Dyer now recognized his wife.

"Take the skiff!" the old man cried out to him, but the Dyer did not hear; he had leapt off the bank into the river and was already on the other side, swinging himself up from the water. The young woman let out a scream of fear when she saw his powerful head surface. She broke loose from her guides and bolted across the meadow. She thought she was still without a shadow, marked by infamy, and now her judge was coming ever nearer. She tried to hide, but there was neither tree nor bush anywhere. He was closing in by leaps and bounds with arms open wide, and from his lips there poured an uninterrupted cry of love and tenderness. She could feel him right behind her, and when she turned around to measure how far ahead of him she was, she saw her shadow flitting along behind her. She flung her arms in the air for joy, whereupon the shadow's arms also rose up and touched the Dyer's knees, so near was he. She stood breathless before him as her heart nearly forced her to the ground. He pressed his hands together before his chest and bowed to her. She dropped down in front of him like a stone; her forehead and lips touched his feet. Her whole self was packed into the sob that burst out of her as she subdued everything in a gesture of humility, so that she compacted her all into the shadow on which she was lying.

Tears poured streaming out of the Emperor's eyes; just as the Dyer's Wife had flung herself down before her husband, so he knelt in the dust before his wife and hid his twitching face against her knees. The Empress knelt down to him as well; for her, too, weeping was something new and sweet. For the first time she understood the bliss of mortal tears. They lay there entwined; as they both wept, their mouths glistened with tears and kisses.

Meanwhile, the old one, the man garbed in white, had neared the skiff from one side, the fisherman and his wife from the other. The old man boarded, while the fisherfolk waded toward it from higher up. The water now came up past their chests. Standing deep in the water, they fetched up wonderful things out of it and handed them to the old man in the skiff—shimmering fabrics, metal vessels and implements, large many-colored birds and fruits in large baskets and creels, as if down below there were mines, forests, and orchards their hands could reach into as they pleased. The old man had trouble stowing it all as they kept reaching their fully laden arms up to him; the skiff filled up quickly and almost capsized, but it grew larger as the old man kept quickly pacing from one end of it to the other. Soon it was as large as one of those barges for transporting salt that sails out from the mountains toward the plain, and it was now abundantly freighted with household goods to furnish in magnificent style a large, three-storied manor house with two wings and with sumptuous fowl, bright-colored fish, and fruits, enough to supply for a year a high-vaulted larder built over living water and outfitted with gigantic hanging rods and hooks.

The Dyer had lifted his wife from the ground with a powerful grip around the middle of her body; it was like an untamed caress, and he heaved her over his head so that she lost her breath and her heart skipped a beat. He was carrying her high aloft like that toward the river bank. Since he was carrying her over his head, he threw it back to look at her and caress her unceasingly with his gaze; under her weight, he lifted his knees like a man who wanted to dance, so that she grasped his thick hair and held tight. Faint cries of fear and happiness kept escaping her at the same time that tears were coursing down her cheeks. Hardly had he neared the bank with his many-colored burden than the skiff, so richly laden and drawing deep, came toward him from the other side with a mighty surge of water, while the fisherman and his wife swam alongside it. The old man had stayed on the opposite bank. The Dyer tossed his wife onto the piled-up carpets and then leapt onto them himself; at once placing his left arm around his wife again, with his right he seized the powerful rudder, placed there from behind by the fisherman. So it was that they journeyed downriver on the Nurse's mantle. The skiff shimmered in every color of creation, and the Dyer sang as no one had ever heard him sing before—not his parents, not his neighbors when he was still single, not his young wife in the thirty moons of their marriage. On one bank the old man and the one in the blue scale armor were looking on and the fisherfolk on the other, while the skiff, rising ever higher, left a golden trail in the glistening water.

High above the river the falcon was circling. The Emperor's glance was drawn more to it than to the splendid ship. Higher and higher the bird soared into unreachable heights as radiant chasms of the sky revealed his wings; the Emperor's glance was far beyond anything like inebriation, though all his limbs were exhilarated through the nearness of the magnificent woman he was nestling in his arms. Sky was above him and below him. Through parted eyelashes he followed the falcon's flight, and over toward the north, where the hills stood darker and more somber, he saw his retinue gathering. He spotted horses, dogs, falcons, and a tall sedan chair swaying along like a chamber of delight surrounded by flames as the sun flashed on its golden trimmings. The Empress was lying in his arms; as her soaring gaze ranged ever upward, she did not see the falcon in the highest, most radiant reach of sky; instead, she heard a song coming from there. Beyond all comprehension, its gentle words and quiet tone made their way to her from this height to her:

Father, what menaced you,
Look, it has disappeared,
Mother, the fearsomeness
Making you tremble!
But this is our feasting time;
We are the bidden guests,
In secret the hosts, as well,
Now we assemble!

The hovering words sank into her like pearls of dew. Her heart trembled, and she folded her hands across her body; they were now free, for the Emperor had sunk to her feet in a transport of happiness. She scarcely dared try to understand what she was hearing, scarcely dared to fathom it. Nor did she know that from the talisman at her breast the words of the curse had long since been expunged and replaced by signs and verses praising the eternal mystery of the bonds linking all that is of this earth.

THE WOMAN WITHOUT A SHADOW

Libretto

I dedicate this translation to Lorraine Truitt.

A character in a Cocteau film says that time lives
inside mirrors, as we can see if we look long enough.

But that mirror can be a glass through which we see darkly,
because it leaves out vital truths—there is a realm in which
time has no dominion, and you and I have been in it.

The Metropolitan Opera was new in Lincoln Center,
and we were young when we saw *The Woman without a Shadow* together.
It's long, long ago, but the passion, the wonder, the awe, the splendor
could be hours old, not decades long gone.

You have lived with fierce dedication to love and kindness;
I can't think of the empress without thinking of you, of
the sacred moments we've shared, of the times you've ennobled me.

We don't defy the years, then; we let them ripen us.
We don't run from sorrow; we let it ennoble us.

Thank you, Lorie, dear and great soul.
Now we can let Hofmannsthal do the talking.

DRAMATIS PERSONAE

(in order of appearance)

NURSE

MESSENGER

EMPEROR

EMPRESS

VOICE OF THE FALCON

ONE-EYED BROTHER

ONE-ARMED BROTHER

HUNCHBACKED BROTHER

DYER'S WIFE

BARAK

SLAVE WOMEN

FIVE CHILDREN'S VOICES

VOICES OF THE NIGHT WATCHMEN

BEGGAR CHILDREN

YOUTH

VOICES FROM THE MOUNTAIN

VOICE FROM ABOVE

SPRIT SERVANTS

TEMPLE SERVANTS

UNEARTHLY VOICES

FIRST ACT

SCENE ONE

On a flat roof above the imperial gardens.

Dimly lit chambers to the side of the entrance.

NURSE

crouching in the dark

Light on the lake –
A quick, flowing sheen –
As fast as a bird! –
The treetops of night
Lit up from above –
A hand made of fire
Is reaching toward me –
Is it you, Lord?
Look, I keep watch
Over your child
By night, with worry and pain.

MESSENGER

steps out of the darkness, armored, suffused in blue light

No, not the overlord,
I am not Keikobad,
I serve as his messenger!
Of us, eleven
So far have attended you,
Each time a new one as the moon waned.
And now the twelfth moon has sunk:
The twelfth messenger faces you.

NURSE

uneasily

You I have never seen.

MESSENGER

sternly

Quiet: I've come here
To ask you now:
Does she cast a shadow?
Woe if she does!
To you and to all of us!

NURSE

triumphant but restrained

None! By the powerful names!
None! None!
Through her body
Light passes
As though she were glass.

MESSENGER

gravely

Sundered from others
To safeguard the child.
The island on all sides
Awash with black water,
Moon mountains seven
Thrust up from the lake –
But still, wretch, you let them
Abscond with our treasure!

NURSE

She took from her mother
The powerful instinct
Of craving for humans!
Alas that her father
Bestowed on her power
Of self-transformation!
How could I follow
A bird when it's flying?
Or hold the gazelle fast
With only my hands?

MESSENGER

Let me see her.

NURSE

softly

She isn't alone:
He is with her.
There was no single night
Within these twelve moons
That he failed to desire her!
He is a huntsman
And a man in love,
Besides that he's nothing!
At first dawn of morning
He steals away softly;
When stars begin shining
He's with her again!
His nights are her day,
His days are her night.

MESSENGER

very emphatically

For twelve long moons
Has she been his!
But he only has her
For three fleeting days now!
When those are elapsed –
She then will return
To her father's arms.

NURSE

with subdued rejoicing

And I along with her!
O day of great blessing!
But he?

MESSENGER

He'll turn to stone!

NURSE

He'll turn to stone!
That is Keikobad's work
And I bow to it!

MESSENGER

as he is disappearing

Watch over her!
Three days! Be mindful!

EMPEROR

appearing in the doorway of the chamber

Woman, awake still?

NURSE

Wakeful and lying
Across your threshold
Like a dog keeping watch!

EMPEROR

coming forward; handsome, young, in hunting armor;
it is dawning faintly

Stay and keep watch
And wait for her summons!
Your mistress lies sleeping.
I am off to go hunting.
Today I shall venture
Out to the moon mountains
And send my dogs
Over the black water,
Where I found my loved mistress,
Who had taken the shape
Of a pure white gazelle.
And she cast no shadow
And set my heart aflame.
God grant that today
I might find my red falcon
Who back then subdued
And caught my beloved!
Then as she fled me

As quick as the wind
And mocked me in running –
With my horse near exhaustion –
The falcon went darting
Toward the gazelle,
Between its eyes –
And with its strong pinions
Struck at her sweet eyes!
She fell to the ground
And I was right over her
My spear at the ready –
Afraid, she then wrenched herself
Loose from that body,
And then in my arms
Was a woman enfolded! –
Could I once again find him!
O how I would honor him! –
My red falcon!
For I transgressed against him
In the frenzied bliss
Of that first hour:
For when she'd turned woman
Fury rose up in me
Rage toward the falcon
For having dared perch
On her forehead
And slash at her sweet eyes!
And wrathfully acting
I hurled my dagger
Toward the bird and struck him,
And his blood began dripping. –
His look is still haunting me.

NURSE

listening the whole time

My lord, if you're planning
A hunt this extensive –
Will you perchance be away overnight?

EMPEROR

It may be three days
Before I return home!
Watch over your mistress
And tell her my hunting
Is only for her sake
And always for her sake!
For all that I hunt down
With dog and with falcon
And all that falls prey
To my arrow and spear:
Is brought down in her stead!
For deep in my soul
And in my eyes too
As well as my hands
And deep in my heart
She is the quarry
Surpassing all quarries
Without any limit!

He exits quickly.

The sunrise has grown brighter; birds are heard singing.

NURSE

to several servants who had gradually gathered around the emperor

Away with you!
I hear our mistress!
She must not look on you!

The servants exit silently.

EMPRESS

stepping out of the chamber

Is my beloved gone?
Why wake me so early?
Let me lie sleeping!
Perhaps I could dream myself
Back into the light body of a bird
Or a young white gazelle!
Alas that I can no longer transform myself!
Alas that I lost the talisman
In the frenzied bliss
Of that first hour!
How gladly I'd like to be
That quick, nimble animal
Struck down by his falcon – Look! –
Over there, look! –
One of his falcons –
Look – has lost its way!
Oh, take a look over there,
It's that red falcon
That in those days past –

With its pinions widespread –
Yes, it's the one!
O day of rejoicing
For my beloved
And for me too!
Our falcon,
Our friend!
Greetings to you,
Fair bird and bold hunter!
He has forgiven us
And come back to be with us.
He's up in that tree now!
There on that branch –
And oh how he looks at me –
From his wing
Blood is dripping,
From his eyes
Tears are falling!
Falcon! Falcon!
Why are you weeping?

VOICE OF THE FALCON

lamenting

How could I not be weeping?
How could I not be weeping?
The woman casts no shadow
The emperor must turn to stone!

EMPRESS

Onto the talisman I lost
In the frenzied bliss
Of that first hour
Was engraved a curse
Read at the time
Then alas! Forgotten.
But now it comes back.

VOICE OF THE FALCON

The woman casts no shadow;
The emperor must turn to stone!
How could I not be weeping?

NURSE

gloomily repeating

The woman casts no shadow.

EMPRESS

The Emperor must turn to stone!

in an outburst

Nurse, I beg you –
Where can I find a shadow?

NURSE

sullenly

He thought in his arrogance
That he could make you
One like himself –

A time frame was fixed
For him to accomplish it.
But he has not loosened
The knots of your heart;
No unborn child
You bear in your womb.
And you cast no shadow
He must pay the price!

EMPRESS

Woe, my father!
Your hand lies heavy
Upon your child.
Yet I am stronger
Than many another!
Nurse, I beg you –
You know the pathways,
And you are most artful,
Nothing is hidden from you,
Nothing too difficult.
Find me a shadow!
Help out your child!

She falls down before her.

NURSE

sternly

A word has been spoken,
A pact has been sealed!
Mighty names have
Been called upon

And now it is your task
To heed and submit!

faltering under the power of her glance

I might know perchance
How to find you a shadow,
But if it's to cling to you,
Then you yourself must
Go forth to fetch it!
And do you know where?

EMPRESS

Wherever it may be,
Show me the way now
And travel it with me!

NURSE

softly and grimly

Among men and women!
Does that not sicken you?
What humans exude
Is to us deadly vapors.
This house as it towers
Up toward the stars,
Cascades and fountains
Of water thrust high up
In hopes of the cleanliness
Of heavenly realms!
To us, though, their cleanliness
Reeks of rust iron
And clots of dead blood

And rotting dead bodies!
And now to leave here
And go lower yet!
To mingle with them,
Be dwelling with them,
To traffic with them,
Speech for speech,
Breath with breath,
To witness their pleasures,
And bend to their wickedness,
Bow low to their ignorance,
All the while serving them!
Does that not sicken you?

EMPRESS

very decisively and firmly

I want a shadow!

with great emphasis

Day is now breaking!
Take me to them:
That is what I want!

Faint morning light.

NURSE

Day is now breaking,
Humankind's day.
Are you catching a whiff of it?
Is it making you shudder?
That is their sun

For casting their shadows!
A treacherous wind
Comes creeping along,
And breathes on their houses
And tugs at their hair!

dawning gradually

filled with scorn and contempt

So now it is daylight,
Humankind's daylight.
A constant mad hubbub,
Greedy and senseless,
Persistent their striving
With no joy or pleasure!

wild and filled with hate

A thousand faces
Without any features,
Eyes that look blankly
But never see anything –
Misshapen things gawking:
Toads, bugs, and spiders,
They look as disgusting to us as these beasts!
I know very well how to
Weasel among them –
Make myself one of them –
Tricking and fooling them
In their very own houses –
That is my element!
Their souls are thieves' souls –
So I'll sell any one of them
To anyone else there!

I'm a cheat and a liar
Among cheats and liars.
They'll call me their nursemaid
Or even their mother;
I'll have numbers of foster sons
And daughters as well
Crawling like vermin
All over my body!
Just wait; you'll have plenty to see.

EMPRESS

It's true, I am trembling,
But there's courage inside of me
Telling me I must do
That which I'm cringing at!
No other task but this
Seems to me worth
My attending to!
Let us go down to them!

The sunrise flames out.

NURSE

Then let us start down!
Your loyal nurse
You've chosen most suitably,
My daughter, dear child,
Just wait now, just wait!
I know how to flutter
Over their rooftops,
I know how to find a way

Through their hearths and their chimneys
And their hearts' twisted pathways
Their fawning and writhing –
I know all about them!

They make their way into the abyss of the human world, the orchestra portraying their journey downward.

The drop curtain closes quickly.

Scene Two

Transformation.

In the dyer's house. A bare room, workshop, and dwelling in one. Left rear the beds, right rear the one door in and out. Forward the hearth, everything shabby in Oriental style.

Lengths of dyed cloth hanging here and there on poles to dry. Vats, buckets, tubs, cauldrons hanging from chains; large ladles, poles for stirring, mortars for pounding, hand mills; hanging sheaves of dried flowers and herbs, with more lined up along the walls; puddles of dye on the dirt floor; dark blue and dark yellow patches here and there.

As the curtain rises the one-eyed brother is on top of the one-armed brother, choking him.

The youngest one, the hunchback, is trying to loosen the one-eyed brother's grip.

The dyer's wife approaches from the rear, looking for a bucket to dash water on the men wrangling.

THE ONE-EYED

punching the brother lying underneath him

Thief! Take that!
Gluttonous robber!

THE ONE-ARMED

gasping

Drag him off me!
You cur! You'll murder me!

THE HUNCHBACK

Help me here, brother!
They're strangling each other!

DYER'S WIFE

throwing water on them

Rowdies, the three of you!
I'll treat you like wild dogs!

*The woman's actions separate the three brothers, who now get up;
then, crouching on the floor, they snarl at the woman.*

THE ONE-EYED

Will you keep on abusing us,
Intruder, outsider?
Who are you? Only the daughter of beggars.
There were thirteen of us children,
But for everyone needy,
The cookpots were brimful
And steamed with rich odors!

THE HUNCHBACK

Raising your hand to us,
Beautiful woman?
You're only here
To pleasure our brother!

THE ONE-ARMED

Let her be, brother, she's only a woman!

BARAK

The dyer, comes through the door.

WIFE

Out of the house with them!
You, get them out of my way!
Or else I won't stay here
With you any more!

BARAK

calmly

Outside with all of you!
There's cloth to be soaked,
Ten baskets full;
Why are you dawdling here?

The three brothers exit.

BARAK

making a tall pile as he stacks up dyed animal pelts

WIFE

Out of the house with them
Once and for all
Or else out I go.
That's how I'll recognize
How much I'm worth to you.

BARAK

continuing to work

Here's the large platter
They eat from when they're hungry.
And where should their dwelling be
If not in their father's house?

WIFE

spitefully silent

BARAK

as before, without looking up

Once they were children
With clear eyes and straight arms,
And the one had a straight back.
I watched them grow up
In our father's house.

WIFE

scoffing at him

For thirteen small children
The cookpots were brimful
And steamed with rich odors –
Along came the beggars;
There was room for them all!

She puts her fingers in her ears.

BARAK

holding a rope to tie the bundle; stops and looks at her

Yes, food for thirteen –
And if need arises
I'll also provide
With these two hands of mine!

standing up and coming close to her

Will you give me children
To gather at the table
When evening comes?
Never will one of them
Leave it still hungry.
I'll rejoice in their appetite
And in my heart feel thankful
That it was given to me
To care for their needs.

He comes closer and touches her gently.

When do you think
You'll give me those children?

WIFE

turns away and brushes his hand away

BARAK

artless and appealing

What's this? Your own husband
Is standing before you –
Shouldn't he be
Permitted to touch you?

WIFE

not looking at him

My husband before me. Aye surely!
My husband. I know what that means!
Aye surely, I know all about it.
You bought me and pay me
To know what that means.
I'm kept in the house here,
Looked after and fed well
To know what that means.
But from this day forward
I want to know nothing.
I'm rejecting the word
and rejecting the thing!

BARAK

But didn't those women
Those worthy old godmothers
Intone potent chants and charms
Over your body?
And seven times since then
I've eaten of that which they hallowed.
And when you're mysterious
And different from others –
I honor that mystery
And bow low to earth
Before the transformation!
O happiness over me
And glad expectation
And joy in my heart!

He kneels back down to his work.

WIFE

Bleary-eyed women
Mumbling their charms and spells
Have no rightful business
With me, with my body.
And whatever you eat before nightfall
Has no power over my soul.

softly

Three and a half years
I've been your wife now –
And you've won no fruit from me,
Have not made me a mother.
My longing for that
I've cast out of my soul,
And now it is up to you
To cast out desires
You cherish so greatly.

BARAK

with artless solemnity and devoutness of heart

Out of your young mouth
Come harsh words
And defiant talk;
But they are blessed with a blessing
That you could revoke them.
I am not angry with you
But cheerful of heart
As I wait, never tiring,
For the ones who are promised
And surely will come.

*Barak has tied the enormous bundle together and hoisted it up to
the stove; from there he loads it onto himself by bending down and
pulling the end of the rope forward onto his back; he straightens up
with his burden.*

WIFE

darkly, as if to herself

But there will be none
Coming into this house.
Instead some will depart
And shake the dust off their feet.

almost silently

So let it happen today –
And not wait till tomorrow.

BARAK

*nods to her good-naturedly without listening to her last words;
tottering under the heavy burden, he makes his way to the door; as if
to himself*

If I carry these goods on my own to the market,
I'll be sparing the donkey who usually hauls them!

He leaves.

*The wife, now alone, sits down on a bale or a sack lying stage front.
A gliding motion, a sudden twilight, a bright flashing in the air.*

*The nurse, in a garment of black and white patches, and the
empress, disguised as a serving maid, are now standing outside but
have not come through the door.*

WIFE

jumping up quickly

What do you want here?
Where do you come from?

NURSE

approaching humbly, making to kiss her foot

Oh, rare, peerless beauty!
Dazzling fire!
Oh, oh, my daughter, in whose presence are we?
Who is this princess? Where are all your attendants?
How is it you're here all alone in this hovel?

She gets up off her knees diffidently.

Permit me a question, my most gracious mistress.
Was the man we just saw one of your lackeys
Or one of your messengers,
The big man outside, his back heavily burdened,
Burly and thick-set, no longer young,
His mouth all agape and his forehead set low?

WIFE

Deceitful one, I've never seen you
And have no idea how you've skulked your way in here –
I can see what you're doing: it's clear you know well
That man is the dyer, and he is my husband,
And I live in this house with him.

NURSE

leaps up to her feet; as if in extreme astonishment

Oh, my daughter, just look here and marvel!
Is this really the wife of Barak the dyer?
Come closer, my daughter, you have leave to do so:
Take a close look at her cheeks and her eyebrows,
Admire her figure, so lithe and as slender
As a young palm tree, and cry out "Alas!"

EMPRESS

I want to kiss the shadow she is casting!

NURSE

Alas, that she is doomed to bear his children!
And wither away cooped up in this hovel!
How blind is fortune and how spiteful chance!

WIFE

Woe that you've come here to scoff at me!
What are you saying, and why do you keep gawking?
Why are you trying to make a fool of me
In front of God and men?

She weeps.

NURSE

feigning surprise while drawing the empress away

Woe, my child, just let us begone now!
She's sending us forth and does not want our service.
She well knows the secret and only is mocking us.
Away with us!

WIFE

standing up abruptly

What secret do you mean,
Disgusting woman!
By my soul and yours too
What secret do you mean?

NURSE

bowing deeply

The secret of the barter
And the secret of the price
For which you'll acquire whatever you wish.

WIFE

By my own soul and by the Day of Judgment,
I know of no barter, know of no price!

NURSE

My mistress, am I really to believe
That you don't know your shadow here,
That this black nothing on the ground
Behind you – that this nameless thing
Might not be bargained for, traded
For eternal enthrallment
And for limitless power over men?

WIFE

turns to look at her shadow

The crooked shadow of a mere woman,
Of one like me?
Who would pay even the paltriest price
For anything like it?

NURSE

Anything, blessed one,
Some eager buyers will pay any price
When a beauty unspeakable
Such as yourself, mistress,
casts off her shadow,
Is willing to part with it!
Ah! slaves male and female,
Brocades and silk raiment
To stand out in splendor
As you change every hour.
Beasts of burden and mansions
And fountains and gardens
And masses of lovers by night.
Splendor of youth going on
For measureless time –
All this is yours,
O sovereign lady,
If you forfeit your shadow!

She reaches into the flashing light and presents to the wife an exqui-site headband made of pearls and precious stones.

WIFE

This for my hair?
You dear woman, you! –
But poor as I am
I don't have a mirror!
There, over the vat
I'll tend to my hair!

NURSE

If you'll give me leave,
I'll see to the task!

*She puts her hand over the wife's eyes; she herself and the wife
immediately vanish. Instead of the dyer's cottage a magnificent
pavilion has appeared, and we are looking inside it: it is the dwelling
place of a princess.*

*The floor seems to be covered with a carpet in the most beautiful
colors, but these are in fact slave women in the most beautiful
garments.*

*They rise up from the floor now, listening as they retreat backwards
on their knees, and exclaim with beautiful voices that sound like bells
chiming in a carillon.*

SLAVE WOMEN

O mistress, our sweet mistress! Aah!

*The woman enters the chamber through a small door to the rear,
left, led by the nurse. She is almost naked, wrapped in a robe, as
if she were coming from the bath.*

The pearl headband is entwined in her hair.

*With the nurse, she makes her way diagonally through the kneeling
slave women to a large oval metal mirror standing to the front, right.*

She sits down there and looks at herself in awe.

VOICE OF THE EMPRESS

For the brilliance reflected here
Would you give your dull shadow?

VOICE OF A YOUTH

as if in answer

For what's mirrored here I'd give
My life and my soul!

WIFE

O world in this world! Awake, yet I'm dreaming!

As soon as the woman opens her mouth, everything begins to grow pale and fade away.

SLAVE WOMEN

Alas! It's too soon!
Mistress! O Mistress!

The dyer's hovel is back, the nurse as she was earlier, the empress off to the side; the dyer's wife in her shabby garb—the jewelry has disappeared—is clinging dazedly to the nurse.

The nurse and the empress exchange a glance.

WIFE

very agitated

But if I were willing –
How would I cast it off
And give it to someone?
That thing on the ground there,
That thing called my shadow!
Tell me that quickly!
Quickly, yes, quickly!
You clever, good woman!
Tell me now, right away, quickly!

The nurse changes her garment and beckons to the "daughter" to come closer, as if in witness.

The wife can hardly contain her impatience.

NURSE

Has it cost you bloody tears
That you have borne no children to that
Blustering husband?
By day and by night does your heart yearn
To bring many of his small ones into the world?
Should your body be a troop road
Your slenderness a pathway
Trampled to nothing?
Are your breasts just to wither
And your splendor be short-lived?

WIFE

softly

My soul's had its fill of motherhood
Before I've ever even tasted it.
I live here in this house,
But the man can't come near me!
So it's been spoken
And sworn to inside me.

NURSE

To cast aside motherhood
From your body
For now and eternity!
To throw off disdainfully

Burdensome problems
That have not been born!
It's that which is spoken,
That which is sworn to!
You rare woman you!
Torch lifted on high!
O you great sovereign
Hailed among women,
Now you will see, now be a witness:
Mighty names now invoked
And a pact made and sealed
And a summons now issued!
Three days we will serve you
Here in this house, this woman and I;
That is the compact!
When they are over –
From mouth unto mouth,
From hand unto hand,
With deliberate hand
And willing mouth,
You will give up your shadow
And take up the first
Of your joys and you pleasures!
And the slaves male and female
And the fountains and gardens
And the vaults fully crammed
With gold by the ton –

WIFE

interrupting her abruptly

Enough now! Be silent!
My husband's returning!
I hear his footsteps!

somberly

He'll be wanting his supper,
Though it isn't yet ready,
And his bed to stretch out on,

almost without expression

Which I don't want to give him.

NURSE

rapidly

You are not alone:
You have us as servants,
This woman and me.
Tomorrow at midday
We'll enter your service.
And you'll have to greet us
As poor, needy kinswomen.
But just after midnight,
While you are still sleeping,
You'll let us go away
For a short time;
No one need know that!
Now quickly to action!

*A gust of wind suddenly sweeps through the room, which the gradual
onset of dusk has plunged into semi-darkness.*

NURSE

commanding

Five fish from the fisherman's vessel
Into the oil,
and frypan receive them!
Fire, now rouse yourself!
Hither, you bed of Barak the dyer!
And away with all guests
To wherever they came from!

The nurse, giving orders, has placed her hands noiselessly together.

Gleaming, the fish fly through the air and land in the pan, and the fire in the stove flares up.

Half of the marriage bed has separated itself, and to the front a narrower resting place for a single person has appeared, while the wife's resting place to the rear appears draped by a curtain.

While all of this is taking place, the nurse and the empress have silently vanished though the air.

The glow from the fire flickers through the darkening room.

The wife is standing by herself, rigid with astonishment.

Suddenly, and as if in fear, there comes voices sounding from the air, as though from the fish in the pan.

FIVE CHILDREN'S VOICES

Mother, Mother, let us come home!
The door is bolted, we cannot come in!
We're out in the dark and we're frightened!
Mother, alas!

WIFE

*in extreme fear at this unfathomable turn of events, looking all
around, baffled*

What's that terrible whimpering
Out of the fire?

CHILDREN'S VOICES

more urgently

We're out in the dark and we're frightened!
Mother, Mother, let us in
Or call our dear father
To open the door for us!

WIFE

in great fear

Let me find water
To silence this fire!

The fire from the stove grows noticeably weaker.

CHILDREN'S VOICES

dying away

Mother, alas! Your hard heart!

*The wife drops onto a bale stage front, wiping the cold sweat from her
forehead.*

BARAK

*appears in the doorway, weighed down with a basket packed full; to
himself, pleasantly*

If I carry these goods on my own to the market,
I'll be sparing the donkey who usually hauls them!

The wife stands up with great effort, goes to her resting place in the rear, lifts the curtain, and says nothing.

BARAK

moving forward

What a wonderful odor
Of fish fried in oil!
Why don't you come and eat?

WIFE

from the rear

There is your food.
I'm going to sleep now.
Over there is your resting place.

BARAK

takes notice; somewhat unwilling

My resting place here? Who did that?

WIFE

from where she is

Starting tomorrow I'll have here two kinswomen.
I'll make them a resting place here at my feet.
They are my handmaidens. So it is spoken
And so it will be.

She draws her curtain.

BARAK

resignedly taking a piece of bread from a pocket and eating it as
he sits on the ground

They told me
Her talk would be strange
And her deeds odd at first.
But I'm taking it hard
And can't enjoy eating!

VOICES OF NIGHT WATCHMEN IN THE STREETS

You married folk here in the city's houses,
Love one another more than your own lives
And know: not for the sake of your own lives
Have seeds of life been given you in trust,
But only for the sake of love itself.

BARAK

turning to the rear

Do you hear the watchmen, child,
And what they're calling?

No answer.

WATCHMEN

You married folk, lying together in love,
You are the bridge across a vast abyss
Over which the dead will enter life!
Blessed be the deeds of your love!

BARAK

listening once more, facing the rear, but in vain; he sighs deeply and stretches out to sleep

May it be!

The curtain falls.

Second Act

Scene One

The dyer's dwelling.

The brothers, carrying bundles, look through the door.

The dyer is loading bundles onto his back, helped by the empress as maidservant.

NURSE

steps to the door and bows down to the ground before the dyer

Come back home soon, master,
For my mistress is consumed with longing
When you are not here!

Barak leaves.

NURSE

walks over to the wife; softly

The way is clear and time is now precious!
How shall I call him who is meant to enter here?

The wife has sat down and loosened the kerchief from her head; her hair is entwined with a string of pearls.

The empress kneels before her, holding out a mirror.

NURSE

My mistress,
Which you are from this day forth,
Give me an answer, please!
What is your wish for me?

Should she bear a message?
Or am I to summon him
With a call filled with longing?
Or someone more mirthful?

WIFE

sharply

About whom are you talking?

NURSE

quietly

About him who is ruling your heart
And for whom you've regaled yourself!

WIFE

calmly

No one dwells in an empty heart,
And I have bedecked myself
For the mirror alone.

NURSE

craftily

I hear and I apprehend
O my mistress!
But I'm speaking of one who's aflame with desire,
Whose knees nearly buckle
In awe and in wonder
When he pictures your hair
As it's caught by a breeze –
You dwell in his fantasies

Though he's never yet seen you.
Permit me to summon him
To this threshold of longing
And perhaps of sweet yielding!

WIFE

standing up

I know nothing of any man
But the one who's just left here.

NURSE

standing close to her

Dear one of my dreams!
The man seen but fleetingly and secretly longed for
Whom you with eyes lowered
Watched closely – and consented to
In your thoughts – treat him with mercy!

WIFE

blushing, in confusion

Who are you, then?
What do you mean to say?

NURSE

quickly rejoicing

We'll bring him to you,
The one who just made you
Turn red so sweetly
As you sent him your thoughts!

WIFE

I can do nothing
But laugh at you!
When I tell you
I just barely know
The name of the street
Where I saw him,
Nor in what part of town,
And not his name, either!

NURSE

But just close your eyes now
And summon him to you!
And then when you open them
He'll be standing before you!

WIFE

still following her own thoughts

I know I was walking
On a bridge, among a large crowd,
With a man coming toward me,
Still almost a boy,
Who passed me unheeding –

NURSE

stealthily grasping a wisp of straw

Broom, impart a shape to me!
And kettle, lend your voice!

EMPRESS

to the nurse

Woe! Must this take place
Before my eyes?

NURSE

softly

A good, sound transaction;
You will gain greatly by it.

She slips over to the wife, hiding the wisp of straw behind her back.

Let your eyes remain shut
But your heart remain open,
You charming one, you!

She throws the straw toward the woman. It flashes up, after which the light remains changed.

EMPRESS

whispering to herself while the wife is thinking out loud

Are all humans like this?
Their hearts so corruptible?

NURSE

Goiters and hernias
Tadpoles and lizards
Are as pleasant to look upon
As all of the rest!

WIFE

her eyes closed, continuing a monologue

– who passed by unheeding;
His look was so haughty –
And yet I still thought of him
On and off, secretly,
As someone to dream about!

NURSE

resolutely

And now it is time;
Come forth, eager overlord!

She claps her hands. A youth is standing there as if lifeless.

Two small, dark figures are supporting him, but they disappear at once.

WIFE

her eyes open now

He is the very same!
And yet somehow not!

NURSE

standing close to the youth, who is gradually coming alive

It's for her sake
That you are here,
Greatly desired one!

hurries over to the wife

What's wrong with you
That you don't recognize him?

WIFE

I want to run away
And hide somewhere!

The youth stands with his head bowed.

The wife involuntarily raises her hands to ward him off.

NURSE

Be quick, lord and master!
And you, mistress, daring!
Terribly fleeting
Is pleasure like this!

VOICES

from the air

Be quick, lord and master!
And you, mistress, daring!
Terribly fleeting
Is pleasure like this!

The nurse walks over to the empress and draws her to the rear.

EMPRESS

breaking away abruptly; listening to sounds outside

Alas! Woe to us! That these two must meet,
The thief and the man who owns this house,
The one with a heart, the other one heartless!

NURSE

coming to the front

Stand apart!
She has the power
To hear faraway sounds
And says that the dyer
Is coming back home!

*She throws a cloak over the youth, and the room grows dark
suddenly; when it is light again, the young man has disappeared.*

*The wisp of straw is lying at the nurse's feet; she picks it up and hides
it in a chink in the wall.*

*The door opens; Barak enters, carrying in his arms a gigantic
copper basin.*

*He is preceded by the one-eyed brother playing bagpipes, the
hunchback crowned with a wreath and hauling a large wine barrel,
and the one-armed brother with a smaller basin.*

Beggar children crowd around the door and make their way inside.

BARAK

to his wife, proudly and happily

Well, princess, what do you say
To this feast? Still feeling finicky?

The wife turns her back to him.

THE BROTHERS

have arranged themselves in a row on the right

Happy the day and blessed the evening!
What all we've bought and are ready to feast on!

Butcher, slice off fresh meat,
Veal and lamb! Let's have chickens, too!
Roast cook, now bring out your skewers!
Come, baker, and show us your best bread,
And devious wine merchant, bring us good vintages!
When we go out shopping, we go at it totally!
Happy the day and blessed the evening!

BEGGAR CHILDREN

joining in

Happy the day and blessed the evening!

WIFE

not looking directly at Barak

All is arranged here
To trample down gentleness.
What's coarse and crude rules here,
And anyone craving bread
Will be handed a stone!
And whoever has sampled
The vessel of dreams
Will be ringed in by animals
And offered the leavings
From the table of jolly folk,
With nowhere to take refuge
Except to start weeping!
These are my words to you,
Lighthearted Barak!

*Overpowered by tears, she sits off to the side and hides her face
in her hands.*

BARAK

putting his bowl on the floor; after a pause of resignation

Eat hearty, my brothers, and let yourselves relish it!
Her tongue is so sharp and her spirit bad-tempered,
But she is not evil –
Her words have the blessing
That she could revoke them
For the sake of her pure heart
And her youth.

*The brothers are hunched on the dirt floor and are bent over the
basin, surrounded by the beggar children; Barak is stuffing choice bits
of food into the children's mouths.*

*Neighbors gather in the doorway—old women, cripples, more
children, and dogs as well.*

BARAK

beckoning to the servant

Look here, quiet kinswoman;
This is for you!
Give some to my wife, too;
She might enjoy sweetmeats
Or a compote with cinnamon.

The empress begins walking over to the wife.

WIFE

flaring up

My slipper across your face;
Stop slinking and creeping!
I mean to taste bitterness

And don't wish to sweeten it.
And I need no seasonings;
Burning with grievance
Over life's treachery
And my dismal fate!

THE BROTHERS
talking back and forth as they eat

Who heeds any woman
And a woman's complaining?
But you've been the patient one
All of our lives!
And always so generous
From when you were born!
Always giving with open hands!
To one and to all!
That's who you are!
Father of us all!

Half drunk, they bow low and kiss the ground before Barak.

BARAK

at the same time as his wife and brothers; meekly, with unintended solemnity

Here are good things for you,
Enjoy them, my brothers,
Be happy as well
That you're home here and living!
That's what you've been granted,
And you're here with me
Instead of the children!

THE CHILDREN

bowing to Barak

O dyer above all other dyers,
And the father of us all!

Scene Two

The drop curtain falls.

The imperial hunting lodge, in a remote part of the forest.

Moonlight among the trees.

*The emperor enters on horseback, dismounts, comes closer noise-
lessly, and hides behind a tree, from which he can keep his eyes on
the entrance and the one fire in the small house. The door is closed.*

EMPEROR

Falcon, Falcon, lost but now found again,
Where are you leading me, wisest of birds?
"The hunting lodge set apart deep in the woods
Must be my dwelling for three days to come –
No one else near me except my nurse,
Far from humanity, concealed from the world" –
So wrote my wife and sent it by messenger,
Her headband entwining
The letter so skillfully.
Now you're leading me
Over mountain and river
Our way leading hither, you strange guide you –
Shall I now hide here in the shadows
As if I were hunting her down still today?
Is that why you've led me here?
Is she asleep? But the house appears empty!
Falcon, my falcon, what can this mean?
Where is your mistress at this hour of night?

Falcon, it seems you have led me here
At an untimely hour.

He listens.

Quiet now, Falcon and listen with me!
Something is coming this way through the air –
Is it the quarry you'll capture for me?
Quiet –

The nurse and the empress behind her enter soaring among the trees,
come to earth, and with a few silent steps are at the threshold.

The nurse opens the door, and they pass into the house, now
illuminated from inside.

EMPEROR

Alas, Falcon, alas!
Where is she coming from! Alas, oh alas!
The reek of humanity clings to her now
And the breath of humanity trails in her wake,
Alas that she could lie to me,
Alas that she now must die!

He draws an arrow from his quiver.

Arrow, my arrow, now you must kill her,
Though she was once my white gazelle!
But ah! when you grazed her
She turned into a woman! –
This is not your task, then; you must not kill her!

He places the arrow back into the quiver and draws his sword
halfway out of the scabbard.

Sword, my sword, it's you who must strike her!

But you are the weapon that loosened her waistband,
This is not your task then; you must not kill her!

He replaces the sword in the scabbard.

But with my bare hands! Alas no!
My hands are unable to!
Woe, woe!
Up now, my horse, and Falcon lead on!
Off with us! Lead me away from this place,
To wherever your spiteful heart
Bids you to go!
To those barren abysses of steep rocky wastelands
Where no man or no beast will hear my lamenting!
Woe, woe!

Scene Three

The drop curtain falls.

The dyer's dwelling. Barak is at work.

The wife and the nurse exchange impatient looks.

WIFE

subdued, to herself

There are people who always have time,
And if the market is shutting down,
They still seem to do just fine.

BARAK

turns his head to her

I'm going soon. It's hot and I've gone at it hard
Since early this morning with not much to show for it.
Would you give me some water, wife?

WIFE

without turning to him

That's what the maids are for.

The nurse pours him a drink, surreptitiously emptying a liquid into it.

BARAK

not looking

Won't you give it to me?

The nurse gives the empress the drinking vessel.

*Stretching out her arm, the wife signals the Empress to hand it to
Barak.*

BARAK

drinking

I'm sleepy. It's hot.

WIFE

impatiently, in a mockingly sing-song voice

Says: I'll go, but just keeps sitting!
Says: I'll do it, then does nothing!
Look at me, the lord of the manor!
If I just have it, then it's mine,
House and hearth and bed and woman!

BARAK

not angrily

I'm very sleepy, must lie down, wife.
Come evening – I'll carry – these goods – to the market.

falls asleep on a bundle of herbs

WIFE

bursting scornfully into song

And sparing the donkey who usually hauls them!
Sparing the donkey who usually hauls them!

NURSE

coming over to her, quietly

Mistress, desist now from shouting and raging!
I poured a strong sleeping draught into his drink!

WIFE

Who told you to do that?

fearfully

Barak! Barak!

She goes over to him and looks at him as he is sleeping.

NURSE

drawing her away

He'll sleep until morning. For now all is well with him.
Many beautiful hours are yours to look forward to.

WIFE

Who told you what I call a beautiful hour?
I want to go out, but you're to remain here.
I don't want to be in your hands as you spy on me
Probing my secrets,
Old snake spotted black and white!

NURSE

My mistress, why venture to seek him outdoors,
Him who awaits you and yearns for your summons?
Allow me to set him right here at your feet;
Just say it openly: he may make his approach!

WIFE

with biting sharpness

If I said it openly and bandied more words with you
We still would be talking about two different things.
He might make his approach, yes, the man I am thinking of –
But nothing from you may come anywhere near me.
That's why I turn him down.

gradually changing her tone

Something about him could come
That you'd never notice:
Something unable to come to me
At *your* hands!

Dreamily, filled with longing

Should a man step onto a shoreline
Intact until then,
There is no wall or bolt
That could ever keep him out.

NURSE

quickly

I'll call him!

Gathering darkness and a flash of lightning.

Holding him by the hand, the nurse leads on the apparition of the youth.

WIFE

You serpent, what have I to do with you
And anyone you bring to me!

YOUTH

in an ethereally high voice

Who's brought it to pass
That I stand so abruptly
Before my mistress?
The power is too great!
The force is too sudden!

kneels and covers himself

WIFE

with feigned severity, not casting a glance at the youth

Who decrees that old kinfolk
Are granted to know
What is none of their business?

affecting contempt as she casts a flirtatious glance at the youth

Bring me my cloak! It is my wish
To ride down the river and delight in the cool air.

making as if to leave

NURSE

goes over to her and embraces her feet; urgently, passionately

Achingly sweet unrest
Drives you hither and thither.
There's nothing you're yearning for
But the yearning for sweetness
Here and now!

As if blowing on the fire, not without the demonic magnitude of a procuress.

Whoever partakes of bliss
Will fear not even death,
Having tasted of eternity
While nonetheless forgetting
The way bliss was reached for!

YOUTH

If I am far from you,
Yet it's your nearness
That's shattering me;
If I'm right in front of you,
You're unapproachable,
And so it's your distance
That's working to kill me!

He falls backward like someone completely powerless.

WIFE

as if unconscious

I had a dream I was flying to you
With unending kisses
Like a dove feeding its baby,
But my dream has now killed you!

She bends over him, trying gently to move his hand away from his face.

His glance meets hers, and his hand reaches out to take hold of hers.

She starts back with a cry as the nurse struggles to lead the empress out the door with her.

WIFE

suddenly transformed

Woe is me. Where are you going?
You traitors! Come back here and help me.
If the dead are alive
Can the sleepers be dead?
Wake up, my husband!
A man's in the house!
I need you! Wake up! Come help me!

She hurries over to Barak, shakes him, and sprinkles him with water.

The nurse is on hand to help her.

NURSE

throwing her cloak over the youth

God protect us
From this foolish young woman.
It's all right; don't worry!
The wind can shift quickly
And we'll call you back!

BARAK

waking from his stupor, sitting up

How could I sleep so sound? Who's shaking me now?

WIFE

You shouldn't sleep in broad daylight!
Should be guarding your house
From robbers and thieves

And looking out for me!
If something like this
Ever happens again,
I'll stay here no longer.
Do you understand?

BARAK

standing up and looking all around wildly

Did robbers try breaking in? Give me that hammer there!
Brothers, come hurrying! Come to your brother!

WIFE

untying the hammer from around his hand

Stop all your yelling and oafish behavior!
Just when you're working you keel right over,
Take leave of your senses and start talking strangely.
Is there something wrong, or doesn't it bother you
To frighten me so with your uncouth, crude antics?

NURSE

aside

How firmly she seizes him,
Saddles and bridles him,
Splendid of her!

BARAK

slowly

Wife, did I scare you now?
Good soul, I'm back with you!

WIFE

mockingly

Back with me. Oh what that means to me!
You're back with me! Such a great joy!
Back with me!

BARAK

trying to gather his tools

Things are happening to me, but I don't understand
them,
And there's some power over me in the darkness –

staring out before him

My best mortar split apart –
Have I lost understanding? Do I still know my handiwork?

WIFE

staring at him hard

You're certainly missing one skill in your handiwork;
Never had it to start with.
If you had you'd stop talking
About yourself and your mortar.
If what just now took place took place in your heart,
It would surge up with tenderness;
You'd fear lifting your hand
Or taking a footstep,
Lest you injure the miracle
You don't even notice.

almost with loathing

But a dumb beast just plods along
The edge of a steep cliff
Not at all bothered
By the depth and the mystery!

BARAK

half to the maid next to him and helping him pick up his tools from
the ground

I hear but I don't know what's being said,
And I spilled all the glue when I fell down so quickly –
And I'm truly afraid when it comes to my handiwork
Afraid of not being able to feed
Those entrusted to my hands.

WIFE

As for feeding myself
You just needn't bother!
And if you should see me
Reach for my cloak,

She does so, both maids helping her.

Perhaps to ride along the river,
Perhaps to stroll next to the gardens
Or anything else my whim leads me to do –
There's a chance that some evening
I won't come home to you.
For today's not the first day
You're hearing my voice
But don't grasp what I'm saying;
The one you think close is in fact far removed,
And you think she's caged up like a captive bird

That belongs to you,
Bought at the market for a mere pittance,
But she's elsewhere, I tell you,
At home somewhere else.

She prepares to leave, summoning the nurse to go with her and the empress to stay behind.

Barak is looking on, distressed and bewildered.

The wife and the nurse leave by the door.

The empress is on her knees, close to Barak, and is gathering together the tools scattered on the ground.

BARAK

only now noticing that he is not alone

Who's there?

EMPRESS

looking up at him

Your servant, my master!

Scene Four

The drop curtain falls.

The empress's bedchamber in the hunting lodge.

The empress is lying on the bed, sleeping restlessly.

Wrapped in her cloak, the nurse is sleeping at the foot of the bed.

EMPRESS

still asleep, not opening her eyes

Look – Nurse – look.
The man's eye; you can see his deep anguish!

as in a dream, solemnly

Before such a gaze even cherubim
Fall on their faces!

after a silent moment, starting up abruptly, her arms outspread

Barak – against you – I have transgressed!

She lies back down and falls asleep again, more soundly now.

The wall of the bedchamber disappears, and there is a view into a mighty cavern with an opening to the outside.

Here and there dim lamps faintly illuminate ancient burial niches carved into the basalt.

To the right can be seen a bronze door leading to the interior of the mountain.

The cry of the falcon grows audible. Then the emperor, as if following the falcon,and feeling his way with his hands, enters the cavern through the opening.

The empress writhes in her sleep and moans softly.

The emperor takes one of the lamps; it shines out brightly in his hand, so that he catches sight of the bronze door.

A rushing sound now comes from behind it, as if of falling water.

VOICES

from inside the mountain, luring—threatening

luring

To the water of life!

threatening

To the threshold of death!

luring

Draw nigh!
Have courage!

threatening

Woe!
Shrink back!

The emperor goes toward the door.

The falcon flutters around him, emitting piteous warning cries.

The emperor pounds on the door, which opens and admits him, then closes again.

VOICE OF THE FALCON

The woman casts no shadow,
The emperor must turn to stone!

The cavern disappears; the lamps in the empress's bedchamber burn more brightly.

EMPRESS

Woe, my husband!
What a path you must tread!
But where to?
And all through my doing!
The door slammed shut
As would a grave.
He wants to come out
But is sealed in forever.
His foot loses motion,
His body grows numb now.
His voice silent, smothered
And only his eye
Can cry out for help!
Woe, my nurse,
how can you sleep!
Both men are doomed now
Through my dire offenses –
For the one, no more help,
For the other, destruction –
Barak, alas,
I kill all I touch!
Woe to me!
I would sooner myself
Be turned into stone!

Scene Five

The drop curtain closes.

The dyer's dwelling. The room is in twilight and grows ever darker.

BARAK

sitting on the ground

In the middle of the day it's turning dark
So that I can't see to work.

The three brothers enter with lowered heads.

It is dark outside as well.

BROTHERS

Something is wrong, but we don't know what,
Brother!
The sun has set in the middle of the day,
And the river's not running, won't flow any more,
Brother!
Things are happening to us, but we don't know what!

They break out into howling and moaning, which lasts some time.

NURSE

with the empress off to the side

Mighty powers are at work,
My mistress,
And something is menacing us.
But we will call upon
Powerful names,

And that will come to pass for you
On which you have set your heart!

EMPRESS

to herself

Alas, how the world is filled with so many sons of Adam!
And alas, that I came into it only to worsen their heartache
And to ruin their happiness!
Praise to him who saw to it
That I should find this one man among the rest,
For he shows me what true humanness is like,
And for his sake I want to remain with men and women
And breathe their breath and bear their hardships with them!

BARAK

to himself

It feels as if my hands are tied together
And a heavy stone is lying on my heart,
And in my soul a hint of everlasting night.
Praise to him who's never known the darkness
And whose eyes have never shut,
Unique among the rest!

WIFE

to herself, on the ground off to the side

How can I stand it in this house
And not put an end to it –
Where there's darkness in the middle of the day
And the dogs are howling in fear
And no one puts them out!

a pause

WIFE

*leaping up, fixing Barak with an evil glance, then walking back and
forth without looking at him*

There are people who always stay calm,
And no matter what happens, no one ever sees
A change come over their face.
Day in, day out
They trudge like cattle
From barn to trough,
From trough to barn.
They don't know what has happened,
Don't know what was meant by it.

*a flash of bright lightning; the brothers begin howling; the wife
stamps her foot with rage*

WIFE

continuing

They can only be hated for being like that,
And whoever belongs to them,
Given into their hands,
Can only be ridiculed.
But I am *not* in your hands.
Do you hear me, Barak?
And when you have left the house
To carry your goods on your own to the market,
Then I'll summon my lover, prepare to receive him,
A stranger among strangers!
And when I awaken you out of your sleep
I'll just then have risen from his embrace!

another flash of lightning; the brothers cry out again

Do you hear me, Barak?
Make them be quiet
So that you understand me!
I don't want you to be a laughing-stock
To your kinsmen;
I want you to *know* instead!
I did all of this here in your house
For three long days
But my pleasure was tainted,
For I thought about you all the while
When I should have been forgetting you,
But I kept seeing your face
Where it should never have been!
But now it has come to me
How to escape you
And tear you clean out of me;
I know how to do it now!

Barak stands up abruptly; his brothers lurch to his side.

I cast off from my body all children,
Never to be born, and my womb will be barren
To you and all others.
Rather, I'll give myself
To the winds and the night air,
My home here but elsewhere.
And to serve as a sign
I have bartered my shadow
To prosperous purchasers,
And the price is magnificent,
Truly incomparable!

BARAK

in extreme rage

The woman's gone crazy!
Light a fire
So I can see her face!

The fire flares up.

BROTHERS

The woman casts no shadow;
So what she said is true!
She sold it to keep
Her unborn children away from her body!
Her shadow is gone from her,
So now she is without one,
Woman accursed!

NURSE

to the empress

Up and away;
Take the shadow;
Snatch it up quickly!
She spoke the words clearly
And knew what she was saying,
So it's accomplished now!
The solemn court of the stars
Can't undo the transaction!

BARAK

breaking free with terrifying violence

Brazen face of a whore
And yet you look so lovable,
Have you no trace of shame?
Hurry to me, Brothers; bring me a sack,
And I'll fill it with stones
To drown this trollop
In the river
With my own hands!

making for his wife

BROTHERS

holding on to Barak

No blood on your hands, Brother!
Drive her out of the house instead
Let the fate of a stray bitch be hers
Creeping in ditches and gutters!

BARAK

at the same time; still trying to seize hold of his wife

My eyes are all clouded,
Help me, my brothers!
Bring me a sack
And fill it with stones,
So I can drown her
With my own hands!

BROTHERS

holding on to Barak

No blood on your hands, Brother!
Keep your hands clean, father of ours!

BARAK

at the same time

If you won't help me
I'll trample you down!
In my soul I have sworn it
And I'll carry it out
With my own hands!

Just as he stretches his right arm upward, as if swearing an oath, a gleaming sword hurtles through the air into his hand.

Even combining their strength, Barak's brothers can barely hold him back.

NURSE

to the rear with the empress, her eye unwaveringly fixed with demonic pleasure on the spectacle; at the same time as Barak and his brothers

Who cries for blood
But is unarmed
Receives a sword
So others are harmed!
Dark blood flows fast;
And they're aghast
But ours the shadow,
Ours at last!

EMPRESS

*at the same time as all the others; tearing herself away from
her nurse and turning her glance upward*

I do not want the shadow:
There is blood on it;
I will not touch it.
I raise my hands
Into the air
To remain untainted
By human blood!
I call down upon me
Names from the stars,
So as to save her,
Come what may!

WIFE

*in speechless horror at the effect of her blasphemous words, she
has fled toward the left; gradually there takes place inside her a
tremendous change; pale as death but now transfigured, with an
expression she had never shown before, she advances toward Barak
and the fatal sword blow; at the same time as all the others, but
dominant at moments*

Barak, I have not
Done it!
Not done it yet!
Listen, Barak!
My mouth was
A traitor to me,
Before my soul
Did the deed!

If I must die
Before your face,
If I must die
For what did not occur,
Then be quick,
Mighty Barak,
Stern judge,
Noble spouse
Whom I never saw before,
Then, Barak,
Kill me quickly!

*Barak lifts the sword, which is flashing in his hand and sending
out sparks of lightning that sporadically cast light into the room,
since the fire has died.*

BROTHERS

at the same time; hanging on to Barak with the last of their strength

They'll hang you in chains
And beat you
With heavy sword blades;
Take pity on us, father of ours!

*Just as Barak draws back to strike a blow, the gleaming sword
suddenly stops shining and seems to be snatched from his hand.
A low rumbling sound causes the room to shake; the ground opens
up, and through the collapsed side wall the river comes flooding in.*

Meanwhile, the brothers have rushed outside for their lives.

*Barak, and his wife unconscious at his feet, begin sinking
downward, each one separately.*

NURSE

Mighty powers are at work!
Come with me!

The curtain falls quickly.

Third Act

Scene One

An underground vault, divided by a diagonal wall into two parts.

In the right one Barak is seen, darkly brooding and sitting on a hard stone; his wife is in the left part, weeping, her hair loose.

Neither knows the other is nearby; they cannot hear one another.

The wife flinches.

In the orchestra are heard the voices of the unborn children, as in the first act.

WIFE

Quiet, you voices!
I did not do it!
Barak, my husband,
if only you could hear me,
Only could believe me
Before I die!
I wanted to leave you,
You, a man I never
really saw before!
I wanted to forget you
And thought I could flee
From your sight,
But your sight
Stayed fixed on me –
If only you could hear me,
Only could believe me –
I wanted to forget you –
But thought of you always,

And when I followed
Forbidden paths,
There was your face –
It came to me
And searched for me
Before I did that deed in my soul!
A stranger –
I summoned him
And led him on,
And we grew close –
But not completely –
Barak, Barak,
I woke you, didn't I,
Don't you remember?

BARAK

to himself

Entrusted to me
So I could care for them,
Keep them safe in my arms
And hold them dear
And treat them gently
For her young heart's sake!

WIFE

sometimes together with him

Serving and loving you
As my ways of yielding:
If I could just see you!
Breathing! Living!
Could give you children, good husband! –

BARAK

Entrusted to me –
But toppling to the ground,
For fear of death at my hands!
Woe! If only I could see her once more
And could say to her:
"Don't be afraid."

silence, and then

VOICE

from above, on Barak's side

Up, on your way upward, man,
The path is clear!

At the same time a ray of light from above falls into Barak's cavern;
the steps of a spiral staircase hewn into the rock become visible.

Barak stands up and begins climbing the stairs.

WIFE

Barak, my husband,
Stern judge,
Noble spouse!
If you were again
To menace me with your sword,
I would want to see you
By its glinting light
Even though I would be dying!

A ray of light from above falls into her cavern; the brightness in
Barak's empty chamber has vanished.

THE SAME VOICE

now on the left

Woman, on your way upward,
For the path is clear!

The wife hastens on her way.

*The caverns sink down. Clouds appear, and when they break up,
they reveal a flat expanse of rock like the one seen when the
empress lay sleeping. Stone steps lead from the water upwards to
a vast temple-like entrance into the interior of the mountain.
Dark water that has made a channel in the rock is flowing on the
opposite side.*

The door to the middle entrance is open.

On the top step the messenger is waiting.

Spirit servants left and right.

*A rowboat with no one guiding it is now making its way along
the water.*

*The empress is lying asleep in it, the nurse kneeling next to her,
holding her close, looking out nervously to see where the boat is
headed.*

The messenger has been waiting for the boat to arrive.

It comes to a stop.

SPIRIT SERVANTS

Here they come now!

MESSENGER

Away!

*He steps back inside the mountain, as do the spirits, and the bronze
door closes behind them.*

The empress awakens.

*The nurse attempts to hold her back, using her free arm to push the
boat away from the bank, but in vain.*

The surroundings grow brighter.

The empress rises, looks around, and tries to step onto land.

NURSE

hastily pushing her down, agitated

Away from here!
Help me loosen the boat
From the rock!

quietly

Mighty powers
Are toying with us!
Of its own will
This thing cobbled together
Of evil wood
Kept forcing its way
To this horrible place.
If my wits weren't sharp
What would become of you?

EMPRESS

The boat wants to stay here –
Can you not see that?
The stairs, look!

NURSE

*gives up trying to push the boat away from the bank, driven by
feverish impatience*

Let the boat be, then!
But away from here fast!
I know the way;
Moon mountains seven
Tower around us,
This is the highest one,
a frightening region!
Tuck up your skirt now
And be quick of foot:
I'll lead you below
And find a way out!

reflecting, searching

I saw this entrance gate
Once long ago.

Trumpet calls are heard, as if from the interior of the mountain.

EMPRESS

Do you hear that sound?
It's a summons to judgment.

quietly, somewhat apprehensively

Is it you, O my father?

Keikobad! Speak!
It's been long since I've seen him,
But one thing I know –
That he loves to solve quandaries
And scatter all darkness
As he sits on his throne
Like Solomon.
His seat is on high
And his wisdom inscrutable –

artlessly and courageously

But I am his child
And I am not afraid.

*The nurse, afraid, is looking off to the side to see if she can find
a way out.*

The trumpets call again, louder.

EMPRESS

her hands raised, filled with fear

My lord and master!
They're sitting in judgment on him
Because of me!
Whatever binds him
Binds me as well.
Whatever he's suffering
I choose to suffer too.
I am in him,
He is in me!
We are one.
I want to go to him.

turns and prepares to walk up the steps

NURSE

filled with fear

We must be off!
I'll procure you a shadow.
So it is settled,
And so it is sworn!
You'll stay the same,
My sweet little daughter,
As through your body
Passes the light –
Though that woman's
Pathetic shadow
Has now fallen to you,
And it clings to your heels;
So you seem to be like her
And yet you are not.
So you still are conforming
To what was determined!

with flattery

Keep on with your lover, then,
Bestow your caresses!
I'll help you to find him
And I'll bear up with patience
When I see him embracing you
Year after year
While I stay a she-dog
Cooped in his house!

sighing with resignation, not strongly

Woe is me!

But we must be off from here!
Away from the threshold;
To set foot across it
Is worse than death!

EMPRESS

So you know this threshold?
You know, then, where
This gate opens onto?
Answer me!

NURSE

To the water of life.

EMPRESS

Answer me!

To the threshold of death!
So cried out the voices.
I demand that you tell me now!
You grasp the mystery,
Know what's at stake here.
Answer me!

So sly in your silence?
Going to such lengths
To darken my mind

To baffle my insight?
Light shines inside me, though,
Light shines before me!

passionately

I must go to him!
Water of life,
I must feel it on me,
Must sprinkle him with it –
Water of life –
Is it the blood
From these veins?
Let it pour forth
So that I may awaken him!

She turns with a decisive movement toward the entrance.

NURSE

flinging herself down and grasping the empress's garment

Have pity!
You're entangling yourself:
A thousand nets,
Mirages and phantoms!
Horrible trickery!
Water of life indeed –
Gruesome deception.
If I have to offer
My own heart's blood,
I'll keep water away from you,
From your heart and your soul!
Water indeed leaps up
Inside the mountain,

Tall golden columns
Rise up from the ground!
Water of life indeed:
All those of our kind,
Descended from spirits,
Who so much as wet their lips –
Are imbibing a hopeless doom
Worse than mere death itself,
Appalling, unspeakable,
Atrocious catastrophe.

The empress has made her way up to the top step.

NURSE

in extreme fear

Don't you hear me?
Terrifying
Is Keikobad!
What do you know of him?
You are his child
And have given yourself
Into human hands
And squandered your heart
On a body corruptible!
Terrifying
Will be your penalty
When you fall into his hands.
And he thinks that no outrage
Is greater than this:
To dally with hated ones
And consort with those cursed!
Woe unto her

Who gave you birth,
And let seep into your blood
The yearning for humankind!
Woe unto you!

EMPRESS

transfigured, decisively

Out of our deeds
Judgment arises!
Out of our heart
The trumpets resound
With their clear summons. –

resolutely, holding her hand out to the nurse, decreeing

Nurse,
I part from you
Now and forever.
The needs of humanity
You know all too feebly,
And all of the mysteries
They aim for in spirit
Are hidden from you.

very solemnly and nobly

How high a price they
Pay for everything,
Out of crippling guilt
Renewing themselves
Just like the phoenix,
Raising themselves
Again and again

From perpetual death
To perpetual life –
They themselves barely know it,
But you not at all.
It's to them I belong.

powerfully

I am not of your kind!

*She goes to the entrance, which opens noiselessly; she enters, and it
closes behind her.*

NURSE

*wants to follow but does not dare venture farther; on the steps;
despairing*

The needs of humanity?
Treachery is the meat and drink
They hunger and thirst for.
She's deceiving herself!
A curse on all of them!
Their endless trudge forward
Into sheer emptiness,
Their greed so insanely
Tied up with fear –
Trickling their poison
Into the crystalline soul
Of my child!
A curse on all of them!

It grows dark, and a red fog begins rising.

BARAK'S VOICE

in the wind

Ah!

WIFE'S VOICE

from the opposite side
Ah!

BARAK'S VOICE

If I could but find her!

WIFE'S VOICE

lamenting

O my beloved one!

BARAK'S VOICE

Do not fear anything!
Look here, just look!

WIFE'S VOICE

at the same time

Find me,
Kill me!

BOTH

Alas, alas, oh alas!

NURSE

Humankind! Humankind!
How I despise them all!
Squirming like eels,
Screeching like jackdaws,
Polluting the earth!
Death be upon them all!

BARAK

from the right, calling into the fog

I'm seeking my wife; she keeps running away from me!

recognizing the nurse; filled with fear; pressed hard; nearly moaning.

Have you not seen her –
My kinswoman?

NURSE

pointing upward to the left

There – over there!
There – up there!
She is cursing you
Unto death!
Punish her –
Take revenge –
Hurry now!

BARAK

exit left, moving upward

I'll go to her! Go to her!

WIFE

appearing from the left, lower down

You – You – where is my husband?
You – I want to go to him!

NURSE

pointing to the right

There! Over that way!
Waiting to kill you
With his own hands.
Save yourself,
Run!

WIFE

rushing off to the right in the wind and fog; with fierce resolution

Barak! I'm here!
Strike with your sword,
Kill me quickly!
exit right; it grows darker

NURSE

Woe to my child,
Now at their mercy,
Mirages before
Her very eyes.
Traps and snares
At her feet!
She's gone inside!
She'll drink! The golden

Liquid catastrophe
Passes her lips
And burns its way down!
Her face
Horribly twitching,
A human cry
Forced out of
Her wounded throat!
To come to her rescue
If I have to die!
Keikobad!

She makes for the entrance.

MESSENGER

coming out of the gate; staunchly

The name of the mighty lord?
To whom are you lifting
Your voice, wretched cur?
Be off with you!
Back from the threshold!
Clear off now, forever!

NURSE

as if insane with turmoil

Entrusted to me –
You yourself, messenger!
Three days long!
I looked out for her,
I struggled with her –
She then cast me off –

She no longer knows me –
Keikobad!
He must listen to me!

tries to walk past the messenger

MESSENGER

barring her way; staunchly

She now stands before him!
Who has any need of you?
No one.
Go your own way!

NURSE

Keikobad!
Your servant
Cries out to you –
Punish her, but
Do not dismiss her
Unheard!
Only admit me;
I'll explain all my actions!
Keikobad!

The fog grows thicker as it continues rolling in; thunder and storm grow more vehement.

It is growing darker and darker.

At the same time the voices of the dyer and his wife resound through the storm as they call out to each other and search in vain.

MESSENGER

forcefully; with a trace of contempt

Who are you
That you should call on him?
What do you know
Of his bidding
And why he has imposed
An ordeal on her?
When he charged you
To guard his child,
Did you have no suspicion
He might have wanted
Her to run away from you?

more and more terribly

Still he casts you aside
Through all time to come
For being unable
To guard and protect her!

BARAK

invisible

You, where are you?

WIFE

invisible

You, where are you?

BARAK

Don't run away!

WIFE

Find me!

BARAK

Come to me!

WIFE

Come to me!

BARAK

Just to see you – breathing, living!

WIFE

Children, husband – loving, giving!

BARAK

Woe, all's lost!

WIFE

Woe, all's wasted!

BARAK

These hands – !

WIFE

Woe, so young!

BARAK

Forgiving you, bringing new life to you!

WIFE

Loving you, bowing to heed and serve!

BARAK

Woe to me, lost!

WIFE

Take pity!

BARAK

Dying! Dying!

WIFE

Woe to us lowly ones!

BARAK

Entrusted to me
So I would care for you,
And keep you safe
in these arms.

NURSE

Let him smite me
In his wrath!
I must go to her!

MESSENGER

He smites you thus
With his wrath
That never again
Will you see her face!

NURSE

Woe, my child!
Lost to me!
Plagues and destruction
Upon all humanity –
May fire eat up
Their very bones!

MESSENGER

with contempt

Henceforth to wander
Among humankind
Shall be your lot!
To dwell now and always
Among those who disgust you,
To mingle their breath
With you own
And always anew!

She pushes past the messenger, trying to move away.

MESSENGER

seizes her forcefully and hurls her down the steps

Onward now, rowboat,
Carry this woman
Down past the moon mountains.
Take her to humankind!

NURSE

May fire eat up
Their very bones!

Once in the boat, she collapses; the boat looses itself and moves away quickly.

Her piercing cry keeps reechoing.

MESSENGER

pitilessly

You've ravaged yourself!
These are your just desserts
According to law!

lightning, thunder, trumpets, and trombones

VOICES OF BARAK AND HIS WIFE

Dying! Dying!
Woe to us lowly ones!

Scene two

Transformation (no curtain).

Gradually, but not to the point of giving a completely clear view, the interior of a temple-like chamber is revealed.

One of the alcoves, the middle one, is draped.

The empress, alone, rises from below.

Spirit servants, carrying torches, come toward her in the darkness.

FIRST SERVANT

Reverence!

SECOND SERVANT

Courage!

THIRD SERVANT

Fulfill your destiny!

They disappear.

VOICES OF BARAK AND HIS WIFE

carried inward from outside, but becoming weaker and weaker, as if doors were being closed

Woe is us, lost!
Take pity!
Dying! Dying!
Woe to us lowly ones!

EMPRESS

going to the curtained alcove

Father, are you there?
Are you threatening me
From out of the darkness?
Here, look on your child.
I have learned
To give myself
But have not bargained
To gain a shadow.
Now show me the place
That is rightfully mine
Amidst all those
Who cast a shadow.

A fountain of gleaming golden water surges up from the ground.

EMPRESS

taking a step backward

I stand in no need of
This golden fountain,
Water of life –
To gather more strength!
Love is within me,
And it is greater!

VOICE FROM ABOVE

Only drink, loving creature, from this life-giving water!
Only drink, and the shadow of the woman it clung to
Will now be your own, and you'll be like her!

EMPRESS

But what will become of her?

WIFE'S VOICE

from outside

Barak!

BARAK'S VOICE

from outside

Where are you?

WIFE'S VOICE

Alas, where?

BARAK'S VOICE

Come to me!

WIFE'S VOICE

I'm searching in vain!

BARAK'S VOICE

Woe! We are lost!

EMPRESS

Barak's voice!
The look in his eye!
All through my fault
Here just as there,
There just as here!

empress shuddering

I have called down
Names from the stars
To remain untainted
By human guilt!
There is blood in that water,
And I will not drink it!

The water recedes completely.

I will not shrink back, either!
My place is here
In this world.
Here I incurred guilt,
Here I belong.
Wherever you are
Hiding in darkness –
There is light in my heart
Enough to reveal you!
I demand my tribunal!
Show yourself, Father!
Step forward, my judge!

The light behind the curtain grows brighter and brighter, its power finally becoming so great that the curtain turns into a transparent veil.

In the brilliantly illuminated alcove the emperor is sitting on a throne carved from rock.

He is rigid, petrified, and only his eyes seem alive.

EMPRESS

spoken

Alas! Woe!
My beloved one stone now!
Buried alive
Inside his own body!
The guiltless guilt
Of my very being –
But he bears the punishment
Because he too deeply loved
The mystery he chose me for –
His loving heart
Mercilessly
Sacrificed
To my mystery!
The knot of my soul
Not untied
By human hands –
Turned to stone now the hand
That did not untie it –
Heart now petrified
By my hardness!
My destiny
His guilt!
Woe to you, stars,
That you treat
Humans like this!

In despair she moves closer to her petrified husband.

To die with you,
Stand up, awake!

Eye in eye,
Mouth on mouth,
Made one with you,
Now let me die!

*She wants to go over to her petrified husband and embrace him,
but she cannot bring herself to.*

*As she moves aside once more in fear of the gaze trained on her,
his eyes follow her the whole time.*

EMPRESS

in extreme agony

Don't look at me so!
I cannot help;
I cannot!

Covering her eyes with her hands, she collapses.

*The statue is glowing in the dazzling light, its eyes directed to the
empress in silent entreaty.*

UNEARTHLY VOICES

muffled but threatening, as if rising from deep chasms

The woman casts no shadow
The emperor must turn to stone!

The statue turns dark, like lead.
*Before the empress's feet the gleaming golden water once again
surges up.*

VOICE FROM ABOVE

Only say, "I will!" and that woman's shadow
Is yours!
And this man will stand up, alive once more,
And go with you!
But you must give the sign; lean forward and drink!

EMPRESS

lying on the ground; struggling fiercely; speaking

Do not tempt me,
Keikobad!
Let me die
Before I yield!

BARAK'S VOICE

outside
Nowhere is help!

WIFE'S VOICE

Woe, to die!

EMPRESS

*rises to her knees, as an agonizing cry like a groan is wrenched from
her lips; in intervals come the words*

I – will – not!

*As soon as these words become audible, the water recedes, and the
chamber begins glowing with light from above after a brief darkness.*

The empress has unconsciously stood up and is now casting a strong shadow diagonally across the ground.

The emperor rises from his throne and begins coming down the stairs.

EMPEROR

"When the heart made of crystal
Shatters with a cry,
The unborn, like starlight,
Come down from the sky.
Wife looks toward husband;
As her mortal shadow is cast
From hips, head, and hair.
Then a dead man may rise
From his own body's tomb –
As heavenly messengers
Come through the bright air
Out of the gloom!"
That was what song I heard
As I was dying.
Now I may live again!
And now come the blessed ones
With singing and dancing
And new life conferred –

The light coming from the dome overhead

has become stronger and stronger.

Now the voices of the unborn children are heard coming from above.

SEVERAL

Hear us as we call out "Father"!

OTHERS

Hear us; we are crying "Mother"!

SEVERAL

Mount up to us!

OTHERS

No, we'll move downward!
Every stairstep leads to us!

EMPRESS

pointing upward

Are those cherubim
Lifting their voices?

EMPEROR

from the bottom step

Those are the unborn
Flying toward life, toward us,
With wings as red as dawn;
They were nearly lost
But now these strong ones
Are rushing toward us
Like starlight.
You have conquered your fear;
Now messengers from heaven

Show the unborn children
How to draw near!
Their way is now clear,
And they're hastening on!

He has stepped down from the bottom step.

The empress moves toward him while pointing upward, as the light from above grows ever brighter.

As a silver sound makes a prelude to the unborn children's song, she kneels down.

Facing the empress, the emperor likewise kneels.

The unborn children begin singing as the empress and the emperor hide their faces in their hands.

UNBORN CHILDREN

from above

Listen and heed our voices,
Struggle and bear up strong,
So that our whole lives long
Each of us rejoices!
Whatever afflictions
You've suffered with fortitude
Become for us gleaming crowns
Earning our gratitude.

The emperor and empress stand, looking upward with delight.

EMPRESS

joining hands with the emperor

They are angels singing to us!
Their strength is what they're bringing to us!
Not yet born, exposed to dangers,
Not yet anchored, with no aim,
Hear them call us, not as strangers.
Since we're together, they're winging to us!

EMPEROR

Not at rest yet, not secure;
They have no anchor – still unsure.
No place yet, but as they're flying
Let it be to us they're plying.
Hear them call us, not as strangers.
Since we're together, they're winging to us!

They hold each other in an embrace.
Bright clouds surround them.

SCENE THREE

Transformation.

Beautiful countryside, sharply rising, emerges.

In the center a golden waterfall tumbling from a gorge.

*The emperor and empress are seen above the waterfall; they descend
from the height.*

WIFE

from the left along a narrow footpath

If I fail of his love,
Let his judgment then strike me,
Him with the sword.

hurries along toward the abyss

BARAK

on the opposite side

Stand still and I'll hold you,
My arms will unfold you,
My soul-mate forever!

*As she catches sight of him and stretches out her arms, her shadow
falls across the abyss.*

BARAK

rejoicing

Shadow, your shadow
Has led me to you!

WIFE

My only true lover,
I'm wedded to you!

UNBORN CHILDREN

from above

Mother, your shadow!
You look like a bride!
And now nears your spouse
To stand by your side!

At this moment a golden bridge, taking the place of the shadow, falls diagonally across the abyss.

Barak and his wife step onto the bridge and fall into each other's arms.

The emperor and empress, standing higher up, have stepped to the edge of the precipice.

They turn forward, and the dyer and his wife look up toward them.

BARAK

Now I'll rejoice more than anyone's rejoiced!
Now I'll achieve more than anyone's achieved!
For through me hands are outstretched,
Flashing eyes, children's mouths,
And I'm now uplifted
With sacred power!

EMPEROR

*pointing downward toward Barak and his wife and then farther
downward to the world of humanity*

Only from far away
Did the noise sound insane,
But listening close this way,
The sound is humane!
How moving to hear
If we take it in fully,
O wife ever dear!

CHORUS

invisible, joining the jubilation

Brothers and dearest ones!

THE TWO WOMEN

Each casts her shadow
Impelled by desire,
Both of us steeled
By chastening fire.
Near to the brink of death,
Killed and not killing,
Mothers of children since
We became willing!

Veils drop down, concealing the landscape and the characters.

VOICES OF THE UNBORN

in the orchestra

Father, what menaced you,
Look, it has vanished,
Mother, your fearsomeness
Past now and banished!
Now this is our feasting time;
Each is a wecome guest;
But in secret a host as well,
Blessing and blest!

Curtain.

ABOUT THE AUTHOR

HUGO LAURENZ AUGUST HOFMANN VON HOFMANNSTHAL
(1 February 1874 – 15 July 1929) was an Austrian novelist, poet, dramatist, narrator, essayist, and librettist–most notably for several of Richard Strauss's operas. Not a few of his peers considered him a genius. Hofmannsthal began publishing lyric poetry and plays while still a student and eventually became a leading figure in Austrian culture, going so far as to maintain a government post during World War I. An artist with a great sensitivity to truths both harrowing and beautiful, he prophesied the trials of the Western world and, as the Habsburg empire collapsed, deepened his commitment to the European tradition.

ABOUT VINCENT KLING

VINCENT KLING is a translator and scholar of German literature who teaches at La Salle University in Philadelphia, Pennsylvania. He has translated fiction, poetry, and criticism by Heimito von Doderer, Heimrad Bäcker, Andreas Pittler, Gert Jonke, Gerhard Fritsch, Hugo von Hofmannsthal, and Aglaja Veteranyi. He was awarded the Helen & Kurt Wolff Translator's Prize in 2022 for his translation of von Doderer's *The Strudlhof Steps*.

ABOUT DANA GIOIA

DANA GIOIA is a poet, critic, and former Poet Laureate of California. He is the author of six collections of verse, including *Interrogations at Noon* (2001), which won the American Book Award, and *99 Poems: New and Selected* (2016), which was granted the Poet's Prize. His critical collections include *Can Poetry Matter?* (1992), which was a finalist for the National Book Critics Award, and *The Catholic Writer Today and Other Essays* (2019), whose title essay started an international debate about the role of faith in contemporary literature. His most recent books are *Poetry as Enchantment* (2024) and *Weep, Shudder, Die: On Opera and Poetry* (2024).

Gioia has written five opera libretti and edited over twenty literary anthologies. For six years he served as Chairman of the National Endowment for the Arts where he launched the largest programs in the agency's history, including Poetry Out Loud and the Big Read. Gioia has been awarded 11 honorary doctorates. He has also received the Laetare Medal from Notre Dame, Aiken-Taylor Award in Modern Poetry, and Presidential Citizens Medal. Gioia served as the Judge Widney Professor of Poetry and Public Culture at the University of Southern California where he hosted the first Catholic Literary Imagination Conference in 2015. He lives in California.